PRAISE FOR KAZ DELANEY
&
MY LIFE AS A SNOW BUNNY!

"Jo is a hilarious new character. A must-have book."
—Erika Sorocco, teen correspondent
for the *Press Enterprise*

"This book is refreshing and perfect reading for any teen. . . . Very enjoyable!"
—*RT BOOKClub*

"*My Life as a Snow Bunny* is a wonderful book that I'm sure you will love!"
—*Romance Reviews Today*

RED ALERT:
HOTTIE AT TEN O'CLOCK!

The old pickup slid to a halt, spraying us with more red dust. Like I needed that. I was just getting one of my best withering looks into place when the driver poked his head out the window.

And smiled.

And all the breath left my lungs.

He was gorgeous. Drop dead deliciously gorgeous. The sweetest eye candy I had ever seen. Finally. A true Aussie hunk. A knight in shining armor on his trusty—*or was that rusty* (but like, who cared!)—steed come to rescue me. It was fate. This was no accidental meeting. It was meant to be. . . .

PRINCESSES DON'T SWEAT

Kaz Delaney

SMOOCH NEW YORK CITY

SMOOCH ®

June 2004

Published by

Dorchester Publishing Co., Inc.
200 Madison Avenue
New York, NY 10016

ISBN 0-8439-5325-X

The name "SMOOCH" and its logo are trademarks of Dorchester
Publishing Co., Inc.

Printed in the United States of America.

Visit us on the web at www.smoochya.com.

Q: How can I possibly thank all the people who made this book a reality?

    a) Dedicate my life, donate body organs and put all my life insurance policies jointly in the names of the best agent (Michelle Grajkowski) and best editor (Kate Seaver) in the world?

    b) Throw myself in awe at the feet of Leah Maxwell (a.k.a. Leanne McMahon)—the title queen?

    c) Dedicate my eternal gratitude and service to the best crit group in the world (Valley Girls) for their over-and-above-the-call-of-duty diligence?

    d) Bless the gene pool that I have brilliant children (Paul, Melissa, Kim and Ree) who provide great inspiration, and especially thank Ree for all the late night reading and cool advice?

    e) Dedicate it all to my best friend and husband, Rob—who in his own way makes it all possible?

A: All of the above. Thank you, I love you all. (Okay, you got me. Maybe I was just a bit hasty about the insurance policies. . . .)

PRINCESSES DON'T SWEAT

Prologue

Question: What do you do if your mom does a complete one-eighty over a guy she meets in an Internet chat room and the guy is, like, a trillion miles away in Australia and she wants you both to leave New York City and go meet him? At Christmas!

a. Be assertive. Gross out and demand DNA testing to prove she really *is* your mother. Looking for love in a chat room is so totally last year.

b. Be analytical. Show her the stats to prove how many Internet relationships end in disaster. It's a freak show out there!

c. Be smart. Ask your doctor which diseases make it impossible to fly and then read up on the symptoms. Go for one with spots, coughing, and delirium. Fevers are harder to fake.

d. Be organized. Study up on everything Australian and present her with a list of all the things you're positive you're fatally allergic to down there. Make an alphabetical list with "Australia" at the top. Being allergic to a whole country has to be impressive. Will she really put your life in mortal danger for a down-under fling?

e. Be strong. Refuse to go. Ignore all the pictures you found when you were researching of the cute Australian lifeguards sporting big tanned shoulders and wearing those itsy-bitsy swimsuits and little surf caps and forbid yourself to dream about being rescued by one of them. Stand firm. This is your life too.

f. Be savvy. Compromise. Agree to go, but only under certain conditions. Like that you go five-star all the way—and you stay right at a beach, with a balcony suite—and that there are binoculars in your Christmas stocking. Really high-powered ones.

In my experience there is no problem in life that can't be solved by a magazine quiz. No one should ever make a major decision without one—even if you have to write your own. Option "f" had a big check mark beside it. I'd done this quiz weeks ago, and when I'd passed it around to all my friends they'd all agreed with my choice. Okay—so it was a no-brainer because options "a" through "e" had struck out.

Totally failed.

Unlike the permanent marker, which worked really well. Luckily most of the red spots on my body (re: option "c") had almost worn off. I can't believe I actually resorted to such tactics. Like, how juvenile was that! Of course, that totally described my level of desperation.

So I was going to Australia. Mom had won, and she'd cut a mean deal. She was an expert on cutting deals—it was why she earned such big bucks as an advertising executive—so I had to be really sharp about what I wanted. The final draft went down like this:

Madeline (me) would get to lie around the beach and hotel pool in her hot new bikini; order lots of icy, fruity drinks from cute male waiters; drool over all the hot lifeguards and practice fake drowning techniques so as to make full use of their skills. (Mom wasn't totally with me on this one.) Additionally Madeline and Frances (that's Mom) would get to do some fun things together to make up for all the times Frances had to work instead of spending quality time with her daughter during the year. Of course, that included making time for some side trips to major stores to burn a few calories in a heavy credit card workout. (Surely Australia had some good shopping?) In return Madeline would, when asked, spend some time with the Internet guy and be on her best behavior.

Frances (Mom) would spend heaps of time getting to know the Internet guy better and decide if she really wanted to marry him, which so far she thought she did. (Eeowww! She was even calling him her fiancé, but that could have been because I told her that at her age it was totally disgusting to call him her *boyfriend*. (Not that I was happy with her alternative choice.) Additionally, as promised above, Frances would spend some quality time with Madeline—doing some cool mother/daughter stuff.

If all went according to plan, the trip wouldn't be a total train wreck. There'd be some salvageable moments. But, even so, I wished we didn't have to go traipsing halfway around the world just so my mom could hang out with some guy. I was really burning up about the whole deal. I'd never admit it, but I got this kind of sick feeling in the pit of my stomach when I thought of my mom and this guy. He was different from the other guys she'd dated. There hadn't been many, but I'd never seen her go loopy over any of them. Not like she was with Barry. That was his name. Ba-ree. I hated his name, which was totally unfair, since I didn't even know the guy.

She'd already met him, so this was round two for her. After chatting online they'd met up at some business conference in Chicago last spring. This was another reason for me to worry. Mom went off guys really fast, and she wasn't going off this one. This was a bad sign. A waaay bad sign. He was all she talked about. . . .

And I mean "all." It was like I didn't exist sometimes. . . . I felt like putting name tags on all the photos of me in the apartment. Just in case she'd forgotten who I was. Or that I existed.

I've tried to work out how I feel and I think it's just that we've been a pretty good team for fifteen years, Mom and I. My whole life it's just been us. And an assortment of babysitters and live-in help. Fifteen years of sharing Mom with her work. And then this Ba-ree comes along, and not only is he getting Mom's attention, he has attachments. Two kids—thirteen-year-old twins. That meant the tiny bit of time my mom did have free would be divided four ways. . . .

Four ways? And this was something I was supposed to be *happy* about? Hellooo???

"I can't believe you're going to be on a beach for Christmas!"

The quiz I was holding went flying through the air—and I nearly went with it. "Accckk! You scared the life out of me!" I'd forgotten Shelley was still in my room. I'd forgotten she was even in our apartment! To be honest, I wasn't sure why she was. It wasn't like she was my best friend; Reesa had that honor. Shelley and I were part of the same group of friends, but we rarely hung out just the two of us. She'd come over with this great going-away-slash-Christmas gift of really cool underwear, which made me a bit suspicious. It wasn't like Shelley to be generous, and I wondered if she'd copied off my history paper and was having a guilt attack.

She was sprawled across my bed with one leg sticking straight up in the air, her eyes glued to her new Jimmy Choos. Jimmy Choos! They were an early Christmas present from her dad, who'd decided to go skiing in Switzerland for Christmas. Without her. I had trouble with that, but if she did, she wasn't saying anything. The whole time she'd been here she'd done nothing but admire the shoes and talk about them. I was so over it. And no, I was *not* jealous.

"It's not like I have a choice. Mom cut me one of her famous deals."

The leg finally dropped, and I didn't have to look at her dad's guilt gift anymore. She started to roll off the bed. "I don't get you, Madeline. I thought you, wanted a dad. You're always going on about it."

Okay, so everyone has a soft spot, one where if you get kicked there it hurts more. I guess my soft spot was my dad. Or lack of a dad. At the moment, with Mom's obsession with this Australian computer geek, it was worse, and I felt myself tighten up inside. "Excuse me? I do *not* 'always' go on about it! I have never said I wanted 'a' dad—as in 'any' dad. And I've never once said 'anyone will do.' I've always said I wanted *my own* father. I'd simply like to find him. Find out who he is. Introduce him to my mom . . ."

"Man—that is so weird. . . . Like, aren't parents supposed to have met *before* they make a baby?"

"So they didn't. Okay? You wanna make a bigger deal out of it than it already is?"

Shelley backed off. In fact, she kind of backed right out of the apartment, which on one hand was not a bad thing, because I wasn't exactly great company. On the other hand, I felt pretty bad I'd chased her away. Then my eye caught the Victoria's Secret lingerie box. . . .

"I never quite trust that girl. Don't know why . . ."

With the box still in my sights, I had to agree. The words had come from behind a huge stack of laundry. Pattie came up to my shoulder, weighed twice as much as me, and was nearly four times older than me, and she was probably the closet thing I had to a grandmother—and my best friend. Well, her and Reesa. The fact that they were aunt and niece just made it more totally cool. Kind of like a twofer. She and Jake took care of the apartment—and they took care of me when Mom wasn't around, when she was traveling around the country or around the world. They had a couple of rooms in the back of our apartment.

I took some clothes off the stack so I could see her face.

"You want a hand to finish packing?" she asked.

"Nah. I'm okay."

She dropped heavily onto my bed and picked up my electronic journal from the pile of things to take. Her eyes were sad as she looked over at me.

I shrugged. "Dad might like to know how the trip went."

She fingered the tiny computer that held the details of my life so far. It was to be a gift to my father if I ever met him. "I'm sure he will. . . ." Then she sighed. "Are you really? Okay, I mean?"

I sighed too and flopped down beside her, watching the early snowfall outside my window. There was no snow where I was going. If that great weather didn't have strings attached, my sunny vacation wouldn't be a bad thing. "What if she really loves it, Pattie? W-what if she really loves . . . *him*?"

Kaz Delaney

Pattie smoothed some hair off my face. "I've heard Australia's a pretty place. It's not hard to lose your heart in a pretty place. But your mom's not silly, Madeline. Trust her. It's only for three weeks. What can happen in three weeks?"

I shuddered. "Are you kidding? In three weeks? Apart from the ever present threat that my mom will do a total flip-out and decide never to come back here—I could be devoured by those horrid monsters they have down there! Have you seen the pictures of those giant poisonous spiders and bugs—and those totally disgusting snakes? Do you even know some of the most poisonous snakes and spiders in the world live down there! And I'm supposed to go there voluntarily? Ugghhhgh . . ." I really did shudder again, this was the stuff of major nightmares. "Come on Pattie—I'm not even good with Lady Beetles. I must be the only kid I know who never had pet mice or hamsters. Wildlife and I just don't seem to mix . . ."

This time she laughed out loud. "Oh Madeline . . . Life is never dull with you around. Trust me honey—it's gonna be okay. You're going to a major city—probably the worst you'll have to worry about will be a sewer rat—and that's no different than New York City!"

"And this is supposed to make me feel better!" I fell back on the bed and tried to focus on the positives. Were there any??? Surely . . . "I guess the bonus would be," I added on a sigh, "that there'll be times when just Mom and I get to hang out. I mean, three weeks off work. Mom's never taken such a long vacation."

8

Pattie's smile faded as she nodded; she knew how hard it was for Mom and me to grab time together—but then she laughed. "Hey—maybe you'll be the one to lose *your* heart! I've heard there are some good looking guys down under!"

I did a mock eye flutter. "I know—and they're all *dying* to meet me. And since I discovered Josh Weiner is pond scum, my heart is completely free. How lucky is that? Not that I intend to give *my* heart away—but breaking a few wouldn't be out of the question. . . ."

She pushed off the bed. "Seems I should be saving my sympathy for those Aussie guys. You're a survivor, Madeline Flannagan. Just like your mother."

I chuckled a bit as she walked out. But only because I knew she expected me to. Inside, that really bummed out feeling was back. If ever I needed to be a survivor, it was now.

The rest of my life depended on what happened in the next few weeks. I felt a bit like war had been declared: me against them.

Chapter One

3:20 P.M., Christmas Eve, Sydney

Australia sucks.

Okay—so some people would say I came with that attitude planted right in my head, but even if I had, so far no one had done anything to change it.

First there was the guy at customs. Hellooo? We're Americans, for gosh sakes! We're the good guys! Remember? But did that make one spot of difference to the gorilla who pawed through my underclothing? Specifically, the parting gift of the cherry-colored lace thong. *And* matching bra. Make that matching *push-up* bra!

Were there no secrets worth protecting? Did the entire country *have* to know even before I'd batted my baby blues at one genuine Bondi Lifesaver that my bra size was in negative figures?

And what about my home waxing kit! Did the guy *re-*

10

ally have to open that tin and *poke* in it? Ugh! As if that wax was going anywhere near my private parts *ever* again! It's not as if the world really needed to know I hadn't had time to do the job before we left. It's not exactly bikini weather where I came from, you know!

I saw the look he sent me. He knew!

How humiliating . . .

That was it. I was over it. I really had tried being nice— I'd smiled and made small talk—but the guy was just rude! I'd had enough. "So I'm hairy. Okay? So I need some serious electrolysis. Happy? Want to send out a bulletin?"

The gorilla still said nothing.

Mom had looked bored. "He's got a job to do, Madeline."

I guess Mom was used to all this customs stuff—but I felt like I'd been violated. Not that anyone cared. Weren't there rules about this stuff? Call me the Christmas-stealing Grinch, but I was not happy. I was hot, tired, and hungry, not to mention in a country I didn't want to be in, waiting to meet a guy I didn't want to meet, with a mom who barely remembered I existed. How bad could it get?

A call came over for a flight leaving for Hawaii. It was boarding in fifteen minutes. "Mom, are you sure you want to go through with this? It's not too late to change your mind. . . ."

"Madeline, we've been over this. I'm getting to know Barry whether you like it or not."

Of course, I hadn't expected her to change her mind—

11

but somehow I just had to make one last attempt. I was sounding tough on the outside, but the sick feeling was worse than ever, and it stepped up a notch when suddenly her face softened.

"There he is! That's him."

"Oh, joy."

Mom turned on me then. "Madeline, I'm only warning you once. . . ."

That shut me up immediately. Mom was being a mom. Not my friend—just a mom. In that moment I wondered if the great vacations we'd had in the past had come to an end. There was a time when we would have totally cracked up over the customs guy. Mom's pretty stiff when she's working, but she used to really let go when it was just the two of us. That was in the PB era, though. Pre-Barry. Things seemed to have changed a lot since he entered the scene.

I watched him walk over: public enemy number one. The man who stood between me and my mother. Tall, thinnish, just a few strands of gray mixed in with his dark curly hair. I looked him up and down—cargoes, plaid-patterned cotton shirt. The guy screamed Wal-Mart. And it showed. Next to my mother's perfectly tinted and streaked orange-slash-blond hair and designer non-crease travel suit, it *really* showed.

Not that he noticed my attention. He pounced on Mom like he was a dehydrated man and she was Perrier. First it was all deep eyes and stupid sloppy grins. Then it was lips.

This totally burned me. How was I supposed to be cool and sophisticated when my mother was playing full-blown tonsil hockey right there in broad daylight? Mothers didn't do that sort of thing! Not *my* mother, anyway . . .

I turned away in disgust. "Eeoow! Get a room!"

She didn't hear me. Why would she? I could hardly compete with that! It was only then that I noticed the kid. A guy kid, and he was looking at me like I was weird. Hellooo? If there's weirdness here it's not coming from *this* side!

I sighed. "Okay. I'm Madeline. You must be Barry's son. Right?"

"Yeah. I'm Jason."

"Don't you have a sister? Like a twin or something?"

He shrugged. "Dee. She decided she'd rather go away on holidays with Grandma."

"Smart girl. I think I'd like her."

Then we just stared at each other.

What now? Oh, what a joy this place was. To think my mother actually paid money for me to suffer this much. She could have left me in school and saved herself a bundle.

In desperation I braced myself and turned back to the sickening display behind me. "That's it. I'm getting a fire extinguisher."

Ba-ree finally stopped publicly sucking my mother's face and turned to me with a sloppy grin. "Hi! You must be Madeline!"

13

He went to kiss me but I was faster. Helloooo?! I'd just seen what that mouth had been doing! No, thanks! Ugh!

"Yeah. And you're Ba—"

"Madeline!"

I pulled a face at Mom. "Barry." I said it so sweetly. It could have been perfect if I hadn't rolled my eyes.

Barry looked uncertain. Like he didn't know what to do next. Pity he hadn't been uncertain a few minutes ago, and I wouldn't have had to experience that stomach-turning slobbering. Oh, great. He still wasn't moving. Should we prime some thinking music?

We finally moved, but if I was feeling miserable inside the airport, outside was a hundred times worse. The heat kind of wrapped itself around you and squeezed so you could hardly breathe. And I'd thought the Caribbean had been hot! Maybe it'd be better once we hit the beach. My skin felt seriously like it was peeling right off. Sizzling. Rub in a few secret herbs and spices and I could have been the Colonel's next delicacy.

My vision was blurring and my head was starting to ache. "I hate to be a party pooper—but is it far to the hotel?"

"The hotel?" Barry's face lit up. "I have great news! I took the liberty of canceling your hotel reservations. Surprise! You're coming home with Jason and me! After all, it's Christmas—and hopefully we *are* going to be family. . . ." He was looking longingly at my mother, who had the grace to at least look stunned for one minute before she started blushing. My mother? Blushing?

14

Me? Any color flooding my face wasn't embarrassment or lovesickness. "You canceled the hotel? You canceled our five-star reservations? You canceled my spa? *You canceled room service?!*"

"Madeline . . ."

"Mom! Do something!" My life was disintegrating before my eyes. "Mom! If you want to make out in public, I'll learn to cope. If you want to play Perfect Match on the Internet, I'll cope. But not without room service! Mom? We had a deal!"

Ba-ree was looking pretty green now. "I'm sorry, Fran. I thought you'd prefer it. I know how you hate all that travel for work, and I thought . . ."

Before I could say anything more, Mom sent me one of those looks where I knew one more word could be fatal. This couldn't be happening! I darted a look at the kid—Jason. He hadn't said anything since we introduced ourselves. How could my mother really expect me to actually share a house with Slow and Slower! And no room service.

"I think that's a lovely idea, Barry," I finally heard Mom say.

Just seven words. Seven little words—and she had just signed my death warrant. My mother the traitor. So much for deals. I felt the stinging behind my eyes; Flannagan women didn't cry—but I was pretty close.

I'd pulled myself together by the time we'd stopped outside their house forty minutes later.

The look on Mom's face spoke volumes. If I wasn't so tired, I probably would have smiled. Maybe Barry was going to do all the work for me. This house was definitely not Mom's style. I could see Barry losing brownie points by the second. I took another look and figured I could slum it. And it really wasn't that bad. Just smaller than I'd expected. Single-story. And ordinary . . .

Barry caught Mom's expression. "I know what you're thinking, Fran, and I should have warned you. The new house isn't finished yet—if you're up to it, I'll take you both up to see it later. We're just renting this place for a while. It's clean and it's not far from the beach—and hey, it's not the surrounds that count but the people. Right?" He paused in his jollying and darted an anxious smile our way. "The important thing is that we're together, right?"

My stomach turned over. Had this guy really said that? Surely Mom wouldn't fall for that?

Suddenly I was the one who was green as I watched Mom turn to Barry. "You're right. Of course. It's the people that count. It's the love we have for each other that counts. . . . And it's quaint. I like it! Let's get inside."

I crossed my eyes and focused on not puking, lip-synching language I'd never expected to flow from my own mother's mouth. *It's the love we have for each other that counts.* . . . Oh, God. The horror. My mother had gone all Hallmark on me.

The front door opened straight into the living room, and it was kinda dark, but at least it was cool. A fake tinsel Christmas tree stood in the corner, and some decorations hung on the walls. That's right: it was Christmas. How did these people remember that fact when it was over one hundred degrees outside? By now I was over everything; I just needed some time away from everyone. Dropping my bags I turned to Barry. "If you could just show me to my room and bathroom I'd like to have a soak."

Barry cleared his throat and shot a funny look at Jason. "Um, son?"

Jason rolled his eyes, picked up my bags, and dragged them into a bedroom with two beds whose décor I could only describe as retro Barbie. Eeooow.

"Oh. How pink."

"It's Dee's room—don't touch her stuff. Bathroom's in there."

Sighing, I opened the door of the cramped, old-fashioned bathroom and did my third double take of the day. For a moment I'd thought I'd be seasick. Green. It was all green. The pukiest green I'd ever seen. Green bath, green tiles, green walls, green floor . . . Shuddering, I dumped my stuff on the only flat surface in the room—the pukey green pedestal toilet seat—and started getting ready.

Bath oil in. Special conditioners, moisturizer on. Puce-colored herbal face mask troweled on and purple-glitter-gel-filled eye cover in place. I was ready. I slipped into the filled tub, pulled down the eye cover, and settled in for a long soak. For the moment I could forget the room was green, forget I wasn't in a hotel, forget I hadn't seen one hunky guy, and try to forget Barry ever existed. . . .

Maybe I'd dream of the gorgeous guys I might see tomorrow.

Maybe even have a snooze.

My eyelids hadn't even started their first flutter when it happened: the loud knocking.

"Are you going to be long?" The Brat.

"Yes. Long. Very long."

"Well, you can't. You gotta get out. I need to go."

"So, go! What do you expect from me? A good-bye kiss? Eowww. Get over it."

"Jeez—are you slow or what? I need to *go*! Now!"

My eye cover almost flipped off of its own accord at that. *Me, slow?* Helloo?

The voice was yelling at me again. "This door doesn't have a lock, you know! I'll just come right in! You've got twenty seconds or I'm in. I need the toilet!" The door rattled.

"Use your own bathroom, moron! Jeez!"

"Listen, Miss Up Yourself. This *is* my bathroom. This is *everyone's* bathroom. This is the *only* bathroom! And I need it! I'm counting. Eleven, ten, nine . . ."

Only bathroom? *Only bathroom!* Our apartment in New York had four bathrooms! And my mother made me sacrifice room service for this! "You said twenty!" I yelled back, trying to push away the eye cover and get out of the water and grab my robe all in one movement.

18

Water splashed everywhere; containers went sprawling in all directions. My hair still had twenty minutes of conditioning! My face still had an hour to bake!

"Five, four . . ."

"Okay! Okay!"

Flinging open the door I went to smirk at him, but my feet were still moving. Both of them together. Without any help from me. Sliding . . . "Ahhhhh—heeelp! Oil! Floor!"

Jason's laughter echoed as he barged past. I was still sliding through the door, which was slammed hard into my back and tipped me onto my backside and sent me sprawling along the rest of the hall!

Hobbling to my room, I knew I couldn't trust myself to face my mother or Barry. Instead I lay on the bed to wait for the Brat to finish whatever he was going to do. Eerk. Now there was a sickening thought. Maybe I'd wait a bit longer before returning to the green valley of disgusting secrets. . . .

Somewhere out in the house Bing Crosby was dreaming of a white Christmas. He wasn't the only one. . . .

"Merry Christmas!"

"Good morning!"

"Christmas . . . ?"

Something was shaking my foot. "Wake up, sleepyhead. We've already spoken to Dee. We're just waiting for you! It's Christmas!"

I opened one eye. What . . . ? Where . . . ? What happened? Mental rewind: taking bath. Brat needed to do something vile. I slipped and fell. Then what? My hand flew to my forehead. "Ohmigod! Did I get a concussion? Did I pass out?"

I heard Mom's laugh. *Mom laughing before midday?* Did Barry do that? Did he make that much difference in my mom's life? A curl of pain twisted in my tummy. "No, you just fell asleep," she said. "Must have been jet lag. You slept all through dinner and church last night. You slept all night! But now it's Christmas—and we're waiting for you."

Christmas. Right. I opened both eyes. Mom was closest to me and looking pretty pleased with herself. My eyes scanned to the right. Ugh. So was Barry.

Darn. He was still here.

Great.

Santa obviously hadn't accidentally packed him into the sleigh and dropped him somewhere over the Antarctic without a chute.

So much for making a list and checking it twice. . . .

Eyes went to move on and then froze before backtracking for a second. Hang on—Mom *and* Ba-ree were both grinning stupidly? Heat flooded my entire body. Oh, no! Don't go there. *Do not go there!* Erase the images!

I sat bolt upright. Well, *now* I was awake!

I could see the Brat now too, but he wasn't grinning stupidly. He was laughing outright. Laughing at what? Me? "Glad you find me so entertaining, Brat. Hang around till I wake up some more and I'll show you my juggling tricks."

That sent him into more gales of laughter. I knew then I was going to have a serious talk with Mom about having Barry's genetic pedigree checked. The kid was loopy.

"W-well . . . at least you won't have to bother about putting on the right makeup!" Now he was doubled up.

How amusing for him. The kid was definitely a shingle short of a roof. "Mom, all I can say is, I hope you used protection."

I looked at Mom and expected her to have some smart comeback, but she was cracking up as well. So was Barry.

"What? Did I grow an extra head in the night?"

That brought on even more laughter. Oh, duh. Like I cared. "I'm going to the bathroom. The one and only bathroom. Do I have to take a ticket?" I went to flick back the covers but found the only covering I had was my robe. I really *had* fallen asleep right after my bath.

Then it hit me.

No!

I hadn't finished my bath.

"Ahhhhh! My hair! My face!" I dived for a mirror. My straight, silky blond hair—aaaccckk! The hair I spent a fortune on! Okay—that *Mom* spent a fortune on! But that *I* spent hours on. *Oh, no!* Gone! Okay—not gone as in bald—but not blond and silky anymore. And not straight! "I'm Marge Simpson! A green Marge Simpson!

21

I hate green! And my face! This stuff is like cement! Help me! Mom! Do something!" I spun on the Brat. "This is *his* fault!

"Honey, it's not that ba—"

"Mom! How can you say that? Look at this!" Barry and the Brat were still laughing. "Great! Wonderful! I have to wear a hat for the rest of my life. *And* a full face mask! And to you people it's funny!" Mom got herself together long enough to push me to the bathroom, where I dived under a shower to try to attempt some sort of rescue mission.

Twenty minutes later we surveyed the damage. Emphasis on the word *damage*. My hair was like straw and stood up at weird angles. My face had big red welts the size of Texas. Everything was twice its normal size. Rudolph would have had nose envy!

"They'll go down," Mom soothed. "Just put this gentle moisturizer on. You've burned the skin. No makeup— let it settle a bit."

"No makeup? *No makeup!* Mom! I am a freak!"

"It doesn't really matter, Madeline. There's only us here. No one else is going to see you." Was this woman my mother? This strange, relaxed, "who cares" woman? My feelings for Barry were growing stronger by the second, and they weren't good. They weren't even close to good.

The man himself, Bad-News Barry, chose that moment to poke his head in the door. What was it about that guy! "Um not quite, Fran. I, er, wonder if you and Madeline would come out to the living room? I have a surprise for you. . . ."

Mom clapped her hands like a kid at a party. I tried not to barf as I grabbed some shades to hide behind. And together we traipsed out and sat on the sofa to face Barry, who was grinning like a circus clown. I did have to admit that the aromas coming from the kitchen were pretty impressive, and it was only then that I remembered the last time I ate I'd been in another time zone. "Oohh. Will this take long? I'm starving."

"Here, have a snack. Dried fruit? Nuts?"

This was the Brat? Acting like a host? Wow . . . Wonders would never cease. Eyes still on Barry, I just grabbed a few things and tossed them into my mouth. Something soft, something squishy, something crunchy. Nice combination. Thankfully quite tasty.

As I munched and waited for the show to begin, the voice was back in my ear. Low and menacing. "Enjoy that? It's an Australian delicacy: sugared cockroach."

"Whaaat! Aahhhh! Ahh!"

I dived to my feet, spitting and screaming as I went. "Water! Mouthwash! Antibiotics! Quarantined! Mom!"

I did hear some shouting and stifled laughter, but unfortunately I didn't hear anyone mention an execution, which probably would have been the only thing that would have satisfied me at that moment. It was Barry who finally calmed me down, gave me some water and

23

his assurances that I hadn't just eaten vermin. Like it mattered now! Helloo? I'd just been tortured! Put under extreme mental duress!

Not that my state of mind stopped Barry, who was determined to have his moment. "Fran, Madeline—I have something to say. You'll note that there are no gifts of any significance under the tree from me for either of you. . . ."

Really? No gift? The cheapskate! I was still really bummed that he could make my mom laugh harder than I could, so he wasn't my favorite person. And anyway, just because I didn't want anything from this man was no reason not to feel cheated! And I did! If he started on another one of his "love is enough" speeches, I'd throw up.

Barry continued. "That's because I have a special announcement. My gift can't be wrapped or opened. . . ."

I knew it.

I wanted to add: *Or returned.* Instead I heaved this deep sigh—*Oh, puleese don't let it be one of those gifts that keeps on giving. Like the potted plant-of-the-month club . . .*

Still, he continued. Could he get to the point? "Drumroll, please: I'm taking you on a holiday to the Outback. To see the real Australia . . ." He laughed again. "And we fly out in two days! Surprise!"

We fly out where? What was going on? And why was it every time that guy yelled "surprise" I reached for a self-destructing weapon? The Outback?

"The Outback?" Like, what *is* something called an outback?

Barry laughed again, and Mom and the Brat started making really excited noises. No one seemed to notice I was almost paralyzed with concern. Or that maybe I was still in shock!

"It's the deep center of Australia," Barry said. "Desert, Uluru . . . 'The Rock' to you. Miles of nothing . . . pure magic."

"Nothing? I don't understand. Like, what's 'nothing'? And what's the magic stuff?"

There was just no containing this guy—he was really high on this trip. "It's just that. Nothing. No stores, no houses, no people. It's just nature—natural. It's a spiritual magic."

"Spiritual?" Okay, blame the fact that I had lived in New York City all my life, and while Mom and I have traveled, we tended to go to other cities. Therefore, I knew nothing about places that had "nothing," and the panic was building. "Spiritual? Come on—like, if I want to howl under a moon or get in touch with my inner self I don't have to leave civilization to do it." It was getting hard to breathe now. "So could you please explain exactly what you mean by 'nothing'? You mean, like, nothing but strip malls like the ones we saw in Oklahoma that time? You know—like no big department stores? Or just beaches and small, quaint village-type specialty stores and markets like in Fiji?"

Barry and the Brat laughed again. "Why are you laugh-

25

ing? I didn't say anything remotely funny." Couldn't they see my panic?

The Brat moved his face in real close to mine. And smiled the smile I had finally recognized as a warning. "We mean *nothing*. That is, except red desert, and crocodiles and snakes and—"

"They're like in zoos and things, right?"

He shook his head. "Uh-uh. They're just there creeping and crawling around. It's their country—we'll be going into their country. Their home."

This couldn't be happening. My heart was racing. "He's kidding, right?"

There was one of those awful silences—and suddenly I didn't care if my eyes were red and swollen. I dragged off the shades and, blinking at the sudden bright light, stared at all of them. "But Mom—I don't even like the zoo! You know that! I'm allergic to all those creatures. I know I am. I know! I am totally allergic to everything that creeps or crawls and can't eventually apply for a credit card. I'll break out. . . ." I heaved in another dramatic sigh. "Mom? Do we have to do this? I mean, the most adventurous thing I do is cross Fifth Avenue at peak traffic time! And you want me to go to places where wild animals could be waiting to devour me? Whole?"

Mom shook her head, her eyes still red from laughing so hard. "Honey, think of it as sale time at Saks. We always say that's a zoo!"

I couldn't believe my ears. "Mom, I really don't think they compare!" Desperate, I went for the thing that I thought would get her only soft spot: fashion. "But this was supposed to be a beach holiday—I don't have one single thing to wear."

She considered the problem for a moment—then she shrugged. "We have two days, Madeline. We'll get something."

I turned back to Barry. "You're going to send me out in public, right now when I'm doing a perfect imperson-ation of a freakazoid?" My mouth gaped open—as open as it could gape when my cheeks had been fattened for Christmas lunch like an overdone turkey. "Do you know nothing at all?" Were my eyes going to be permanently crossed every time I had to converse with this man? "Mom! This is so unfair. . . ." My voice broke a bit, and I swallowed the lump back. "Mom, please? We have to get out of this house. . . ."

Her look was sympathetic, but I knew she wasn't go-ing to budge. Help! This could *not* be happening! "Mom? I thought we had a deal?"

She just stared back for ages before finally looking away. She couldn't hold my gaze; I was shattered. Her voice was low. "I know. But I'm asking you to do this for me."

My own voice was a whisper. "But you always said a deal is like a promise."

She didn't look up, and I caved there and then. Mom had gone back on a deal. That was her business. She was a deal broker—she never, ever went back on a deal. Till now. Till Barry came into her life. Right then I would have given everything to be back at home with Pattie and Jake.

Barry and my mom were full of plans, but I just couldn't sit there. Somehow I got back to my room and threw myself on the bed, fighting thoughts of being home in our professionally decorated apartment with Pattie busy in the kitchen. Maybe if I e-mailed her. I found a connection and grabbed my laptop—only to find mail from her.

To: Madeline Flannagan <ubercoolchick@fiprimus .com>
From: Pattie&Jake <thegraysons@freemail.com>
  Hi Madeline! Broken any hearts yet? <g> Jake and I miss you, but we know you're having a great time. You always do. We're heading over to my sister Laura's for a day or so. She said to tell you Merry Christmas—we'll give her your love.
  Pattie (Can't wait to hear all about Australia!)

A lump filled my throat again. Even if I e-mailed her now, she wouldn't be there. Besides, how could I tell her what a horrid time I was having? She'd worry, and it wasn't fair to do that to her.

There was one from Reesa too. It told me that I was so lucky to be in a warm climate while she was freezing her butt off in New York.

Right. So lucky . . . The lump got bigger and tighter. . . .

Chapter Two

Three days later (one of them called Boxing Day—like, what is *that*?) the plane unloaded us some place called Katherine, two states away in the Northern Territory. It was, like, just about as high in Australia as you could go! The tropical north. The equator was closer than the nearest bathroom! The equator! Helloo!

And still I had not seen one eligible Aussie hunk! What was I supposed to do? Hang a sign around my neck that read, *Hi, there! Gorgeous American girl seeks companion. Inquire within*? Like I was that desperate! And like I actually carried around markers and cardboard.

Besides, did I really want to meet a guy in this place? I was absolutely sweltering. If I thought Sydney was hot, man, this was, like, ten times worse! I saw nothing but heat haze. But that didn't stop me from searching for crocodiles. And snakes. Anything that crawled, really—even in the airport.

Kaz Delaney

Barry interrupted my panic attack by calling out our travel plans. We were going to do this big loop back up to somewhere called Darwin, which seemed to be most famous for a cyclone that wiped it out. Great. And we were right in cyclone season now. Oh, man, I was lovin' this. *Not!*

When the car started up, I shoved my headphones on and turned up Eminem. It zoned out everything.

That was day one. Woo-hoo. It gave me so much pleasure to strike *that* day off the calendar as gone and never to return. So far every journal entry since we'd arrived had begun with the heading, *Weirder and Weirder.* This was going to be no different!

Day two started just as badly and as predicted went downhill with each passing minute. The only positive thing was that the car Barry borrowed from his friend was comfy. Oh, that and the fact that my face had gone down and my hair was normal. And it was kind of weird, interesting countryside we were traveling through.

Barry finally found something. Not that I was overjoyed. A crocodile viewing area. Mom looked excited as she got out of the car. Everyone did but me. Not only did I not look or feel excited, I didn't get out of the car. But even though I didn't want to look, I found myself perched on the edge of my seat watching between the trees. Eeowww. The crocodiles were huge! Prehistoric! And they were, like, totally, totally ugly. So much worse than the pictures in the research book! Aaack! Double aack! They should have been banned just for that alone!

Ugh. I watched them snap those jaws and tear at some disgusting dead animal carcass—and knew I'd have nightmares for the rest of my life.

Scarred forever because my mother discovered a chat room.

When the others returned I was hiding behind the seat with my headphones on and my eyes closed, determined never to speak to any of them ever again. Well, at least until it was time for a bathroom break.

That was probably why we'd stopped before I even knew there was a problem. I pulled my headphones off and yawned. We seemed to be on some track, surrounded by red soil and nothing else. Nothing!

"Why are we here? What's Barry found now?" I held up my hand. "No, don't tell me. It's something else creepy, right? Something to add to the list I'll have to share with my therapist?"

The Brat was frowning. "No, the car has stopped."

"Oh, duh . . . How long did it take you to work that out?"

The Brat pulled a face. "Like, it's broken down, Miss Know-It-All."

"Broken down? Like in, we're stranded here?"

I looked out to where Mom and Barry were talking beside the car. Mom wasn't looking happy.

"Does your dad know anything about cars?"

The Brat squinted. "I wouldn't say it's his strong point."

Great.

I opened the door a crack. "Mom, just call a cab! Okay?" I looked back over to see the Brat banging his head against the interior of the car. "What? What's wrong with calling a cab? New York City is crawling with cabs—it's how everyone travels."

He stopped and looked at me with this *I'm going to be patient with you because you are so dumb* look on his face. Then he spoke. "Read my lips: We are in the Outback. Can you see any other cars? Can you see any people? We can't call because there's no cell reception out here. And do you really think a cab would come out here? Do you really think they even *have* cabs out here?"

I ignored the fact that he *may* have been implying I was clueless and looked around for the first time. Okay, he was right—there really was *nothing*. Just like they said. "Where is 'out here,' anyway? Where are we?"

His face fell. "I dunno. Dad heard the car make a noise and he turned off here 'cause he thought it was the driveway to a property. Trouble is, the driveways to properties out here could be thirty miles long. So we're on someone's property, I guess."

"Well, what are we going to do?"

"Dad says the CB radio thing doesn't work—so I guess we wait for someone to come along and find us. And hope they're not too long. Maybe they'll take us back to their place so we can call for help."

"Ohhh. Okay. That would be okay, right? Better than sitting here in the open, in the middle of nowhere, frying to death." I sat and chewed my lip for a minute. "Someone should be along soon. Surely *someone's* been out to a day spa or to lunch or something and they'll have to return home soon. Even to get groceries." Surely . . . "I hope they've got a pool."

The Brat chose that moment to get out of the car and slam the door. What had crawled up his butt? Like I cared anyway.

But I had to admit the Brat wasn't the only one to have something up his butt when four hours went by before someone came along. Four hours! Four hours of my refusing to pee behind the one tree in sight. I could have died of kidney failure! Or heat exhaustion. Or dust inhalation. Or a snakebite . . . or been eaten by blowflies! Eooww, I hated those little black beasts!

I dived out to tell them they'd taken their sweet time—and my feet had actually made it to the ground when Mom darted me one of her *speak and die* looks.

The old pickup slid to a halt, spraying us with more red dust. Like I needed that. I was just getting one of my best withering looks into place when the driver poked his head out the window.

And smiled.

And all the breath left my lungs.

He was gorgeous. Drop-dead, deliciously gorgeous. The sweetest eye candy I had ever seen. Finally—a true Aussie hunk. A knight in shining armor on his trusty—or was that rusty? (but, like, who cared!)—steed come to rescue me. It was fate. This was no accidental meeting. It was meant to be. . . .

And he'd know it as soon as our eyes met. Prime the music. . . .

He opened the door of the pickup and stepped out. It was all happening in slow motion. Each step took forever. . . .

What to do? Did I bound forward? Did I wait with agonizing patience for him to search the faces before him, looking for something, but not knowing what . . . ?

Life hadn't prepared me for what to do in this situation. An image of another magazine quiz flashed into my brain:

Question: When you meet the totally hottest guy you have ever seen in your life, do you . . .

   a. Be bold. Tell him you're doing a survey for kissproof lip gloss, which you happen to be wearing, and ask him to participate.
   b. Be coy. Tell him you followed the voices and they led you to him.
      (Try not to look too spaced out while doing so.)
   c. Be decisive. Trick him into following you home, then lock him in the basement until he loves you as much as you love him.
   d. Be desperate. Throw yourself in front of his vehicle and refuse to move until he promises to sire your first child or at least have coffee with you.
   e. Be subtle. Engage him in conversation by telling him that for a moment you thought he was that really dangerous guy on *America's Most Wanted*. Then you'll both laugh about it.

34

f. Be cool. Do nothing and wait for his eyes to land
   on you. And then wait for recognition to dawn.
   Wait for him to smile—because you are the
   hottest thing he has ever seen.

I quickly discarded all the options but the last. It made
the most sense. And so I waited. And waited. At least
ten seconds went by and he hadn't even looked my way!

He was still moving in slow motion—damn it. Skip to
fast forward! He was about seventeen. . . . A face and
body tanned by spending his whole life in this delicious
sun. Blue eyes that burned clear and bright. No illegal
substance abuse visible. He had on jeans and this tight
navy blue tank top—which his muscles just *loooved*—
and this kinda cowboy-type hat, which he pushed back
on his head as he walked. Light brown–slash-blond hair
curled damply at his temples.

Then he spoke.

And my heart exploded.

That accent . . . pure poetry.

"Gidday! You folks lost? Broken down? Flying doctor
plane going over saw you and radioed down. Lucky.
Sometimes we don't come up here for weeks."

Weeks! Okay, that was a shock. Weeks without leaving your front gate? The longest I went between trips to
the beauty salon was two weeks. The same for my man-
icurist. Then there was the gym, my Pilates class, piano
lessons, and just general hanging out with friends, going
to coffee shops and stuff. Mom and I ate out at least

twice a week if she was home and had brunch at Sammy's on Forty-seventh every Sunday. In truth I mostly did these things with Mom's friend Kitty, or Pattie and Reesa, because Mom was away so often—but it didn't change the fact that I did them. And then there was shopping, which was a weekly event. Between all this and school, I was actually barely home at all. And these people didn't go out for weeks at a time? This was more than just a bit weird. . . .

These people *really* were different. I had to regroup.

Maybe they lived on a huge estate. You know, with a mansion and guesthouses and a pool, and lots of people—like a minicommunity . . . That would make sense.

Barry didn't seem to care about any of these things and shook hands with the guy, who came around to look under the hood of the car.

After a few pushes, pulls, and other guy car stuff, he wasn't looking happy. Did I care? I could have watched those muscles flex all day. "Looks like you've done a fuel pump."

"Can it be fixed?" Mom asked.

"Yep."

Oh, great! We were all smiling now—even my hero, who'd said his name was Mitch Maloney. Mitch . . . It rolled off my tongue like oiled taffy. Okay, so we still had the issue of his grooming and, like, how often he got to the hairstylist's—but he could fix the car. So I could forgive him his little grooming foibles. He was my hero. . . .

My man.

And just when I thought that nothing could be more perfect, another thought hit me. It sent my mind reeling! Could you believe it! My name was Flannagan. His name was Maloney! We were both of Irish descent! Like, what were the odds? How much more proof would this guy need that we were meant for each other?

Barry started rolling his sleeves up. I mentally told him to take a hike. I didn't want anybody blocking my view of my Mitch at work.

"Okay, so what do we do first?" Barry asked.

Mitch was still smiling. I was in need of a heart transplant. "First?" he repeated. "First we get back to the homestead; then we radio ahead and see if anyone up in Katherine or Darwin has got the part—and then we drive up to get it."

His voice was smooth, yet a bit rough. Maybe like coconut-coated creamy chocolate.

Then the words sank in.

Say again? What? We were still stranded here?

On second thought, though . . . it wasn't as bad as it had been half an hour ago. A bit of extra time in the fascinating Australian outback that I had suddenly grown to hold so dear wouldn't be too much of a hardship. Especially once we got back to his place and I could show off my hot new bikini in his pool.

Barry's voice brought me back to our dilemma. "You mean we can't fix it now?"

If I hadn't still been fighting for breath and waiting for the moment our eyes met across the hood of the four-wheel drive, I'd have laughed at his expression. Poor Barry . . . I smiled. He should learn to accept the little challenges that life offers.

In answer to Barry, Mitch did laugh. And what a sound . . . "Not unless you've got a spare fuel pump, mate."

I just loved the way he said *mate*.

"How long will it take us to drive up if they have the part?"

I held my breath at Barry's question. I could see Mom doing the same thing. Even the Brat looked a bit nervous.

Mitch rubbed his eyebrow. Nice, nice hands. Nice eyebrows. With his eyes and my nose . . . what beautiful children we'd make. "Oh, depends on who's got it. But in our old ute—at the worst maybe one and half."

"Hours?"

"Days."

After that shock, the others got into a conversation about what to do. Me? I had only one thought on my mind: Maybe we'd have to spend the night. It was already midafternoon. I could see it all. A midnight dip, a balmy summer night, palms swaying . . .

And me and Mitch.

Sigh . . .

Suddenly I was all business. If this was the love of my life, bring it on. Let's get it rolling. At least get the introductions over so he knew I existed. I was getting way ahead of him here. Like I was writing invitations to the wedding and he didn't know my name!

Time to bring Mitch up to speed.

Confidently I moved forward and held out my hand, my best Mom-spent-a-fortune-on-braces smile in place. "Hi, I'm Madeline Flannagan. I'm of Irish descent." I added that last part just in case he needed extra incentive to be blown off his feet—and then waited for the explosion of love at first sight to kick in.

And waited.

And waited.

"Oh, gidday, Marilyn. Irish?" he frowned. "It's okay—you don't have to pretend or apologize for being a Yank. We accept everybody out here . . . even Americans." Then he turned to Barry. "If you folks want to get your gear out of the car and pack it into the ute, we'll get going."

The Brat snickered. I stared. *Marilyn? Yank! Even Americans!* That was it? That was the explosion? The big bang? The recognition of the one true love of his life? That was *it*?

Helloo?! He didn't even get my name right!

And to think for one moment I'd even considered choosing option "d." Of course, that was before I remembered I was wearing a genuine Rodeo Drive original white embroidered cotton top Mom had brought me back from one of her trips to LA. I stomped back to the car. I was out of love already. But him? Ha! Soon he'd realize what he had under his nose—but it would be too late! He could suffer.

It was just a pity I couldn't get that midnight-swim im-

39

age out of my mind. I felt myself start to soften. Okay—
I'd probably give him one last chance.

The ride to the homestead was a total nightmare. The
Brat and I and all our luggage were shoved into the back
of the pickup with all kinds of greasy rags and animal
stuff. I simply refused to look under anything. It was one
time when what I didn't know couldn't send me into
therapy.

How humiliating! Was this the way to treat someone
who might one day bear your children? That is, if I *could*
actually bear children after this ride. Did the guy have to
hit every bump on the track?

It seemed to take forever before we slowed and pulled
into a yard. Barking dogs greeted us. Dogs? I always
wanted a pet. A nice French poodle . . .

As I climbed down I looked across at the noise. And
froze. Dogs the size of giant black bears, chained to
thick logs, snarled, baring their fangs at me with a vi-
cious *I'm going to eat you now* growl, drooling this disgusting slime from their mouths to make sure I didn't
miss the message. Suddenly all thoughts of frolicking
with a playful pet on a pristine white rug faded.

And I added killer dogs to my trauma list. I could keep
a therapist in business for life.

A few scrawny chickens wandered over. At least they
didn't bite or maim. Did they? I hopped aside just in
case.

Barry and Mitch started dragging bags from the back

of the truck. The Brat helped. I just looked around, suddenly confused. Where were we? This was like a rundown lot somewhere. There were sheds that were falling apart and this old building that looked like it had been a house once—before people let it fall into ruin. It had a rusty iron roof, which was better than the roof of the porch that ran all the way around the would-be house that sagged and looked like it would fall in any minute.

I heard Mitch say, "We'll just take these into the house."

I stopped and stared after him. "What house?"

I followed his footsteps with my eyes. *Oh, no . . .*

It couldn't be. . . .

I would die. I could not stay here. I could not. . . .

But even as I thought it, a little voice was laughing inside my head. Every time I thought I had hit my lowest moment on this trip, something worse happened.

Surely that wouldn't be the case this time?

It was.

A hand tapped me on the shoulder. Dazed, I turned. It was Barry. "Do you still need to use the toil—er, bathroom, Madeline?"

Still dazed, I nodded.

Then he smiled. And he pointed. 'Well, I think you'll find that's that little tumbledown hut about fifty feet over there beside that big tree. Oh—and do watch out for redbacks on the toilet seat, won't you?"

"R-redbacks?"

"Spiders," he said, still looking too cheerful. "Deadly ones. They love outback toilets."

As he walked away whistling, I had only one thought: What was the current Guinness World Record for holding a pee?

Then another thought dived in. . . .

If someone *did* get bitten by a redback, would that person need to have mouth-to-mouth? I suddenly wondered if I should get that part of my life and affairs in order. Like, kind of a procedure-for-catastrophe will. A what-to-do in case something really bad happened. Like, have it written down that in case of my need for mouth-to-mouth, if Barry or the Brat were the only ones available, then to skip it.

Or should I be more specific and just name Mitch as the only person I gave permission to touch his mouth to mine?

That sounded better. Go with specific. That way there could be no disgusting mixups.

Right—that took care of my eventual recovery.

It still didn't solve the bathroom problem though. . . .

Or the fact that I wasn't speaking to Mitch. Or that he hadn't even noticed.

Chapter Three

I don't know how long I stood there lost in thought, but when I came to, there was only me and the chickens left in the yard. Everyone else had followed Mitch into the building they called a house.

So much for fixing my makeup for my grand entrance!

I stared at the building again, and don't ask me what tipped me off—but I somehow just knew there wasn't going to be a palm-edged pool area out back. Or was *this* the back? How did you tell when there was no road? Not that it mattered. It still equated to the same thing. No pool. No romantic midnight swim.

So much for dazzling Mitch with my new bikini.

And so much for relief from this scorching heat! Everything shimmered, including my brain. Was this heatstroke? Maybe I was going to faint. Oh, God, but I needed to pee so bad first!

The screen door they'd all gone through opened with

a screech that set my teeth on edge. At least no burglars could sneak in. Mom looked out. "Madeline?"

I brushed away the five millionth fly. My aerobics work-out at the gym didn't have this much arm waving, for crying out loud. "I'm dying here, Mom!" I didn't add that it was all her fault. I think she knew. I hoped she did—because it would save my coming back to haunt her.

She strode across the yard toward me. Her gold-and-silver plated Salvatore Ferragamos kicking up red dust onto her white designer slacks with every step. This must be what rock bottom looked like. . . .

"Madeline, stop being a baby! Come in out of the sun."

"I can't."

"You can! These are nice people and you won't treat them this way. They rescued us!"

I looked around the yard. "I guess it depends on your definition of 'rescued'. . . ."

She sighed and I saw "the look" coming. Soon it would be "the voice." I knew how she worked. "Madeline . . ."

Okay, so I wasn't a complete idiot. I knew it had to be better out of the sun—but the truth was, I was having trouble moving. My need to pee had become a crisis. "Mom, I— Aaahhh!"

Mom took one look at my crossed legs and rolled her eyes. "Oh, for crying out loud! Just go to the bathroom!"

I knew then that my lips were connected directly to my bladder, because even trying to speak was pushing me closer to the brink. "C-can't make it . . ."

This time her eye roll was Olympic standard. And her grip on my arms was right up there too. "Get behind that shed! Quick!"

"Mom, I can't!" But even as I spluttered the words, supermom had pushed me sideways and shoved me into a squat.

"It's that or go inside and let everyone see you've peed your pants. Your choice." The woman was a reincarnation of Attila the Hun.

It was so humiliating. Squatting behind a shed out in broad daylight! The shame! This was one thing I was not telling anyone back home. There were some secrets best never uttered to a single soul. Although even I had to admit that after a second or two the relief was so enormous that I kind of forgot to be so embarrassed.

That might have been why I was a bit reckless when I stood up. I heard the ripping sound first. Then I felt the pain. "Ouch!" Then I momentarily froze as reality set in. "Oh, my God! Something got me! Something bit me! Quick, Mom, do something. Get me a doctor! Get the paramedics! Call the fire department!"

I screamed. I hopped. I jumped. I ran to hide behind Mom, who was trying to catch me. I didn't want her to catch me! I wanted her to get me professional help! What if it was a giant redback or whatever they're called? Visions of big, ugly, woman-eating spiders scampered across my brain. Oh, God—it had to be that! Its huge claws must have ripped right through my clothes! Sunk its poison into my tender young flesh! Oh, my God,

45

I was dying, really and truly this time. "It was one of those huge deadly spiders, Mom! I know it was! Prepare yourself. . . . This isn't going to be pretty."

The world was turning black. It was happening. . . . Mom grabbed my arms and held me in a death grip. She was probably too stressed to see the irony of that. "Open your eyes, Madeli—"

"No, Mom." I gasped. "I may not have much time. I just need you to know that I want Reesa to have all the things in my closet. But not the red turtleneck. It makes her itch. And besides, red isn't her color. I don't know what to do with my shoes. Just make sure they go to someone who'll love them."

"For goodness' sa—"

"No! Please . . . This is important."

Mom's tone was dry. "If it's a confession, I'm all ears."

My head hung low. I was too weary now to hold it up without help. "No, Mom, it's much, much bigger than that. Mom? I want you to be the one to break the news to Mitch. Be gentle with him. It'll be hard for him to go on. . . ."

Mom's frown was almost a furrow. "Who's Mitch?" Then her face cleared, but only for a moment before the frown was back deeper than before. She was being so brave. I, on the other hand, was falling into delirium, because for a moment I thought she was going to laugh. "Oh," she said. "You mean Mitch who you just met an hour ago and who doesn't remember your name. That Mitch?"

My mom's amazing. Even right to the last she was fighting this. She was in denial, but I didn't have the heart—or the breath—to tell her. "Three hours, Mom. It's been three hours. But if it's easier for you to see him in that negative light, Mom, then yes, he's the one."

Then she did laugh—a full-throated roar that I had rarely ever heard before. "Oh, for God's sake, Madeline! You tore your skirt on a bit of rough iron on the shed! It wasn't a spider! Nothing bit you! It's a scratch! You scratched your backside."

My head spun back up. "Really? I'm not dying?"

"No!" the most insensitive woman in the world spluttered.

I twisted around. "Oh, no! This is my best skirt! I'm going to sue!"

Mom twisted me back and started marching me to the house. We stepped straight off the veranda into the main room. *Note to self: Drop subtle hints that a foyer can lend such an air of intrigue to even the humblest home.*

Inside was dark and kinda cool. I didn't mean cool in a really, like, *cool* way. But cool as in temperature. I hadn't expected that.

There was a jug of water on the table, and I was so tempted after my near-death experience till I remembered that given the state of the bathroom amenities, I was not going to allow a single drop of liquid to pass my lips till we left.

Everyone looked up. *Everyone* was Barry and the Brat and Mitch, who smiled at me. (Yes, he was in looove. I'm sure I even saw a wink.) And this old guy who looked a little bit like Mitch. Must have been his dad.

"Everything okay?" the old guy drawled.

Mom nodded. "Stan, this is my daughter, Madeline." The man nodded and I nodded back. Nice eyes and smile but . . . eeeoww: ugly nose alert. I hoped mine and Mitch's children didn't inherit it. Was birth too young for rhinoplasty? "I wonder if you have some antiseptic?" Mom continued. "Madeline scratched her fanny on the shed outside and I just want to dab a bit on. . . ."

The old man was half out of his chair, and he stopped dead and just stared, his face bright red and getting redder by the second. He'd started to speak but suddenly went dead silent. He half stood, half sat, frozen in place like a statue, too embarrassed to look at us. Well, good! He wouldn't be surprised when we sued him, then. Obviously he knew that shed was dangerous!

But as I let my eyes take in the room, I saw that everyone in the room had the same look. Except the Brat. He was trying not to choke.

Other than that there was complete and utter silence.

Finally Barry got himself together and leaned down to my mom and whispered in her ear, and Mom swallowed back a giggle. "Oops."

By this time I was totally intrigued. Like, what was going on? Mom leaned over to me to repeat what Barry had said. Even this freaked me out! My mother whispering to me in company? How rude! I didn't hear her properly. "What?"

Mom sighed. "It seems 'fanny' means something else here, Madeline."

"So? Like, what else could it mean?"

She rolled her eyes again, trying to be discreet. "The other bit."

"What other bit? Mom, could you just speak English!"

Mom gritted her teeth. Her eyes glared meaningfully. "The *other* bit!"

I shrugged. "Like, help me out here!"

She looked ready to explode. Her voice *did*—right into the silent room. "Your vagina, Madeline! *Fanny* means your *vagina* here!"

The words hung in the air.

I wanted to die.

Bring on the redbacks. . . . And the bluebacks and yellowbacks and every other color . . . I didn't care as long as they promised a fast and painless death.

Suddenly everyone moved. Everyone in the room was busy. And talking loudly. Everyone was talking loudly—but I don't think any one of them was listening. I stared straight ahead—not even my eyeballs twitched—but I still saw it all in full living color.

Unfortunately.

No one looked at another person—except, of course, the Brat, who was looking at everyone and enjoying himself far too much. In mortified silence I watched them all find things to do, all tumble over each other. If

49

there'd been a hammer handy they'd have started building something. With any luck it would be a trapdoor that
would open up and swallow me.

Under my eyebrows I darted a look at Mom, who at
least appeared a bit uncomfortable herself. Good. No
suffering could be too great. Not that it was possible for
anyone to suffer as much as I was at that moment. My
words, when I could make them come, were spit
through gritted teeth, "Mother! Did you *have* to?"

"Get over it, Madeline. It's not like they didn't know
you had one."

"Well, *now* they do!"

I darted a look at Mitch. How could I face him after
this? How could we begin our wonderful relationship
when my most private parts had been discussed in public? Now I'd never know if our marriage was based on
love or pity. . . . And I had my mother to thank for that.

Thinking of our marriage calmed me down a bit, and I
looked around the room for the first time. A silver tinsel
Christmas tree sat in a corner (hadn't these people heard
of real fir trees?), and some wrapping paper and boxes
lay around. Again I found it so hard to believe that it was
Christmas down here.

The rest was ordinary. It *did* look like someone had
made an effort and it made me wonder where Mitch's
mom was. Despite its quaint country charm, I knew he
and I could never live here. Not that I expected him to argue—he'd be dying to get out of this place.

I was totally ticked off that he was pretending to play

so hard to get, though. Didn't he know our time together was limited? That after today we'd have to communicate through e-mail and text messages until we set the date? I sighed. I supposed that, as usual, I'd be the one to have to push him along. Men! They're such babies.

Relaxing, I looked a bit closer at the place my future husband had grown up. I would never return here—but I thought it was polite to remember it so we could warn our children what they'd been saved from.

It seemed like this was an "everything" room. It was pretty big and ran the entire length of the house from front to back—which explained the great cross-breeze that kept it nice and cool.

I guessed primarily it was the kitchen, though I couldn't see the dishwasher. Strange . . . It also had a couple of sofas so maybe it was the living room as well. But then again, I couldn't see the DVD player or the stereo system. I looked again. Hey—I couldn't even see the teev! Maybe they all had personal ones in their rooms, like Mom and I did. That had to be it.

The activity flurry had settled down and everyone kind of moved back to the table as though nothing had happened. I was glad in one way and yet in another I was totally ticked off. Like, helloooo? Were my private bits sooo easy to get over? They pulled out chairs and plunked themselves down and Mitch's dad was talking again.

Okay—I think I had my answer.

I noted there was no extra chair for me. Make that

double okay! It wasn't like I couldn't take a hint. If *I* wasn't necessary to the planning of our escape from Area 51, then so be it. As long as they did it, I didn't care how. And the sooner the better. I had been deprived of indoor plumbing for too long.

Instead I went to the other end of the room. The breeze coming in through the door felt wonderful—maybe I'd find somewhere to sit out there and wait for parole.

I found a couple of chairs on the veranda. They were covered in red dust, and I had to shake out the cushions before I could sit down. I also took particular notice of anything that might creep, bite, sting, or suck. If it looked like it had flesh on its mind, it was a goner.

Flopping down I looked around. The view here was no different, but it was a bit cooler. The sun was starting to set, and I had to admit the sky was pretty. If you liked that kind of thing. Personally, I feel if you're looking for beauty in the sky, you can't beat a skyscraper. Buildings spoke of safety—the empty horizon seemed so desolate, so foreign. It held so many unknowns; things ready to trip me up—or at least bite me. . . .

I noticed a light way down the road and figured it was another house. A few thoughts crossed my mind about it too, but then I decided it was just too cruel to torture myself; obviously I just wasn't in the right neighborhood for pools and mansions.

It was coming out of that daydream that I sensed someone beside me. Not just *any* someone, either. Only a special someone can send off my hunk-alert radar, and believe me—it was screeching.

"Mitch?"

He handed me a plate, which I examined closely, pleased to see nothing more exotic than a sandwich. "Hungry? I hope you like ham. We get a bit sick of it over Christmas." He leaned over and looked at me more closely. Be still my heart. "You okay, Marilyn? You looked like you were miles away." He settled into the chair beside me. "That sunset's pretty magic, eh?"

My smile was tight. He had such a lot to learn. And the first thing was my name! A horrid thought went through my mind that the guy was slow, but I quickly banished it. He just obviously hadn't heard it properly, and in truth, as long as he said, "I take you, Madeline," at the appropriate moment, then everything would be okay. I shuddered as I imagined some guest named Marilyn waltzing off with my brand-new almost husband. *Note to self: Do not invite anyone named Marilyn to the wedding.* Better to be safe than sorry. "Hi! Um—actually, my name's *Madeline*, Mitch."

He laughed. "Is it? Madeline. Jeez. Great impression I made, eh? Sorry." There it was. That Russell Crowe gravelly voice and that hot, hot smile. And my name on his lips. Of course, I forgave him immediately.

A gurgling started low in my stomach and I didn't think it was hunger, but I bit into the sandwich just the same. The bread was dry and there was no mustard—but apart from that it was okay. I couldn't wait to take him to Katz's—a real New York deli. Now there was a true sandwich.

Munching, I went over what he'd said. How could he have been worried about impressing me? *Oh, baby. I don't think I can remember anyone making a better impression.* I swallowed hard and twisted sideways slightly and sneaked a peek.

And sniffed. I'm big into smells, especially of guys. And it's very practical too. I call it my "smellometer." Any guy I can smell from three feet away—good or bad—is out. I hate guys who marinate—even when it's imported. I like subtle. I like it so that you don't smell a guy till you're up close. And Mitch definitely passed the first test; his scent was so subtle that only now that he sat next to me could I inhale his particular aroma.

And it surprised me totally. I usually go for the sophisticated smell—you know, an understated aftershave or cologne—but this guy was pure outdoors, with just a hint of something almost chemical. And surprise, surprise—my nose was dancing!

I slammed back the deep, soppy sigh that threatened to spill over. This was the closest I'd been to him, and the guy was even hotter than I'd first thought. He was like my very own Aussie-flavored shake. One part Russell, two parts Hugh, one part Heath. It didn't get better than this. Hot guys just didn't get better than this. And the best part was that he'd come out on the veranda to be with me! Not only that—he'd brought me food. He was looking out for my needs, paying special attention to me. This wasn't just a sign—this was a full-size billboard. The guy had practically told me he loved me without even opening his mouth. How cool was that?

I wished he'd say *something*, though. I'd heard about these strong, silent Australian guys. I'd learned about it when I watched a documentary for World Affairs Studies. It compared the sexy factor of all these different guys from different nationalities. I could *not* believe it when Mrs. Hudson made me choose another topic after I'd slaved over that one for days. Weeks even. I told her she was stifling my natural curiosity and hunger for knowledge. She told me I stifled her desire to teach. As if.

Barry could take lessons from Mitch—I'd like *him* to be silent. Barry said waaay too much for my liking.

I cleared my throat and purred in my sexiest voice, "Hey, this was really cool of you to come out here and keep me company." Hint, hint. Nudge, nudge.

This was his opportunity to tell me he'd been trying to get some time alone with me all afternoon. I waited, hugging myself to keep from bursting.

He shrugged. "That's okay. Dad told me to come out and make sure you didn't wander off. Gets so black out here without streetlights and stuff that if you're not used to it you can get lost."

"Your *dad* sent you out here?" My mind reeled. Okay, so the guy needed a prompt. But that didn't mean he didn't want to come! And he could have just come out and told me to be careful and then gone back inside. But he didn't. No, he didn't. He'd plunked himself down within kissing distance and didn't move. The fact that there was no other seat made no difference. I smiled in relief. Whew. Good thing I have a logical mind; otherwise I'd have missed the subtleties of this maneuver. Everything was okay. Yes, he was mine.

I put on my sexy voice again. If we didn't have long together this time, I wanted his memories of me to be all good. "I guess a guy like you can't wait to get away to the big city, huh?"

"Me? Nah. I get enough city life when I go to school."

"You go away to school? How old are you?" Not only would he please me, but he'd please my mother as well! She has forbidden me to marry anyone without an education. As if she has a say!

"School? Yeah, of course I do. I'm seventeen, a senior down at a residential high school in Perth. Mostly kids from rural communities who don't have schools close to them. We're on summer break now. Two months."

I smiled and nodded. Sitting here talking to him was just too dreamy. He seemed older somehow than some of the guys at home his age. More mature. Not as into himself. And so, so hot. If the guy had been wearing a thermometer, it would have burst. "Ouch!" Something stung me. It wasn't, like, really bad, and after my experience this afternoon I just played it cool and brushed it away. It wasn't the first time—and I looked but couldn't see anything crawling on me.

"You okay?"

"Yeah." It was a lie. Was that my nose I felt growing?

"How about you?" he asked. "What's your school like?"

"I go to a private school in New York. Scarsdales. It's pretty strict—we have to wear uniforms, which is so uncool. Lots of really rich kids go there—I'm right at the bottom of that scale, and yet my mom makes a lot of money. Some movie stars and rock stars send their kids there."

"Wow—you know anyone famous?"

I grinned. "Nope. Just kids of famous people, who mostly wish their parents were regular people. It's not really cool having half your classroom made up of bodyguards. It's like having people spying on you all day long." I flicked him another smile. "It's kinda fun helping kids to ditch their babysitters for a while, though—we've got a few scams that usually work."

"Somehow I can just see you doing that. . . ." He laughed and shifted to get more comfortable, but he didn't really say anything else. Still, I figured it was a kind of compliment.

"So how about you?" I asked. "What are you going to do after high school?"

"University. U of WA." His eyes were great, even in the fading light. "I want to do Agricultural Science. Dad and I really have some great ideas for this place."

Oops. Ideas for this place? I'd obviously missed something crucial here. I blamed the distraction of those darned beasties that were stinging me! Ouch, ouch! What was it with those things? Backtrack: What had he said? The guy actually liked living here? Okay—regroup time. This was our first biggie—the first hurdle in an otherwise perfect relationship. But we could work through it. I had faith that love would always win out. "But you won't stay here forever, right?"

He shrugged. "Maybe not here. Maybe another property close by. But here in the Territory, yeah."

The sun was sinking fast now. I'd never seen anything like it. I'd felt it, though—my heart was sinking with the same speed. He was staying here? "And you'll, like, get married here and everything?"

He grinned and it glowed bright and warm in the darkness. That voice dropped lower and rumbled over me. "I hope so. Eventually. Kids too, one day. The hard part will be finding the right girl who wants to live out here with me. It's not an easy life."

His eyes held mine. Oh, God. I forced myself to breathe. What had just happened? Was I just lost in the moment? Or . . . had I just been proposed to? Be still my heart! I swear he was looking straight into my eyes when he said those words. How could I miss it? Was I supposed to throw myself into his arms now or what? Why wasn't Reesa here to ask? She was sixteen and knew all about this stuff. Everything went to Jell-O, including my brain. But I had to know, had to be sure. A wrong answer here could ruin my life forever! My voice was barely more than a whisper. "Did . . . Did you, like . . . like, just propose to me?"

He nearly fell off his chair. Okay—he *did* fall off his

chair. But maybe that was just some kind of ruse, because now he was on his knees! *Oh, Reesa, where are you?* She was missing *the* big moment of my life!

His voice was high now and squeaky. "What did you say?"

I didn't answer. But I did give him my sultriest smile. Mom says it's my constipated cow look, which just goes to show how out of touch she is with the modern sexual woman. (Big hint here—she picked Barry, for crying out loud! How much more out of touch could she be?)

So this was it. The moment. The biggest moment of my life. We just sat and stared at each other, both speechless, lost in the wonder of it all. I would remember it forever. Me looking sultry. Him looking . . . ? Well, it was hard to describe the look on his face. *Fear* was one word that came to mind, but I discarded it.

Then he smiled. And I smiled.

Then he laughed. And I laughed. A bit . . .

Then he roared and started rolling around the wooden veranda floor. And I didn't.

I stopped laughing quite so hard. In fact, when he was still roaring two minutes later, I wasn't even smiling. Not a twitch.

Finally he sat up and wiped tears away from his eyes. "You're a really funny chick! You really had me sucked in then! I thought you were serious! Mate, you should go on the stage or something."

Good idea. Book me on the first one out of town. I laughed then. It was lame. It was false. It was a lifesaving device. It hid my humiliation. I wanted to die. I wanted to disappear. I wanted to leave and never see this place again. Now! This minute.

Then I got mad. Okay—I'd been a bit hasty. And yes, it was true that the guy hadn't actually said the words— and yes, I'd just made, like, the biggest fool of myself that it was ever possible to make. But he'd given me all the signs! And those eyes were looking right into mine. And that voice . . . It's not like I couldn't tell he was totally hot for me and wanted me all for himself forever and ever.

And as if I really believed for one second that he forgot my name? Ha! It was all part of his plan to get me for himself. I'm not sure how—but I'd work it out. Trust me.

A thought struck me that maybe Aussie guys were just different. . . .

Yeah, right. As if.

So why was that thought still niggling at me?

It was time for some space. I went to get up and another one of those beasties got me. That was it; I was over them! "Ouch and double ouch! What are those horrid things?" I shooed at one more. "Get off me!"

He smacked my arm. Ouch again! "It's a *mozzie*. Mosquito. They're pretty fierce out here. Bigger than the ones you'd get in the States. You have to smack them. They suck your blood."

My eyes popped. "All of it?"

He grinned. "Nah, they leave a bit."

I hated the fact that the grin still melted me into a puddle. But I wouldn't let *him* see that. "Right. I'm going inside. I want to find out our plans for leaving."

He screwed his face up. Darn. Even that was cute! "Oh, geez! I forgot to tell you. You're staying here a few days"

"We're what? I'm *what?*"

"Yeah. Dad has to drive your mum and Barry up to Darwin to get the part for the car. There's no room in the ute for all of you, so you and Jason are staying here. With me."

With him?

With the traitor? With the guy who thought marrying me was the biggest hoot in the entire universe?

"Ouch!" This time it was him yelling. He rubbed his arm where I'd just smacked him. Hard.

"Mozzie," I said—and kept a straight face. Then I walked back into house to plan cruel and unusual punishments for all the people in my life who were responsible for its total destruction.

Barry was hit number one!

I was so going to enjoy this. . . .

Chapter Four

Back inside I strode straight to Mom, who was sorting our suitcases in what was probably Mitch's parents' room. The décor was unbelievably cheesy. "Eeoww. What is with that totally gross striped and floral wallpaper?"

The air in here was no better. It was worse, thick and sticky. No human could possibly live like this! Surely these people had heard of air-conditioning? If I'd had the strength I would have screamed; as it was, it was possible it would be my last breath. "What's this stuff about leaving me here? Mom? Why do you both have to go? Let Barry go. It's a he-man thing to do. Let him trek out into the wilderness and fend for his family!"

"You know why we made this trip, and it wasn't for a sightseeing vacation. I have some big decisions to make, and I can't make them with Barry four hundred miles away and me down here. The idea was to be together."

I did the whole eyes-wide-open thing. "And this is my

fault? For this I have to be punished? Mom! You are abandoning me. Me? Your own flesh and blood. Aren't you worried about my safety? What if I internally combust?"

"You'll be safe, Madeline—these are good, honest people." Why was my mother always so calm? So detached. So . . . impossible to manipulate!

"How can you be sure? And what about the mysteriously missing mother, huh? Like, where is *she*? Notice no one has mentioned her?"

"Rona's gone to take care of her sister's young children in Broome in the next state. Her sister was rushed to hospital with a burst appendix two days before Christmas. Satisfied?"

I folded my arms in frustration. "Well, that's a likely story! How do you know she's not buried out here somewhere? Huh? How do you know? I could be next!"

"Don't tease me, Madeline. You're making it sound all too appealing."

"Sometimes I think you don't care about me at all! There are authorities I could complain to, you know."

"Save it for Jerry Springer." She stretched toward a pile of clothes. "Pass me that Dolce and Gabbana shirt. The pink-and-orange one."

That stopped me. "You're taking my Dolce and Gabbana?"

"*My* Dolce and Gabbana. The one I haven't had a chance to wear yet because you've barely had it off. Make sure Jerry hears that one."

"*Mother!* You're not taking this seriously! You're leaving me here in the wilderness! Well, what about my *moral* safety? Did you even *think* about that? What if someone tried to take advantage of me?"

She didn't answer straightaway, and for a moment I thought she'd already heard that Mitch had practically left me standing at the altar before we'd even learned each other's last name. Considering I was still coming to grips with the guy's betrayal, I didn't need Mom's opinion as well. And given my delicate nervous state, I also didn't need to hear the *You've only known him five hours* lecture. If true love was judged on how much time people have to get to know each other then the wedding chapels in Vegas would be out of business. Right?

She finally sighed. "If by 'someone' you mean Mitch, then to be honest, I'm more worried about *his* moral safety than yours." She stopped moving stuff from a big case into this little overnight bag and stared me straight in the eye. "I hope you're not going to do anything stupid, Madeline. We've spoken about this. . . ."

Barry walked in then, pretending not to listen, but I could just about see his ears flapping. I felt the heat burn through my cheeks. "Mom! You don't mean—"

"Yes, I mean *sex*, Madeline. You and I have discussed this before, and you know my feelings on the subject. I am trusting you not to do anything irresponsible."

"Er . . . perhaps I'd better leave." That was Barry, and they were the only sensible words I'd ever heard come out of his mouth. If he meant "leave permanently," they would be perfect.

I went to thank him and shove him out the door when the she-devil spoke again. "Not at all, Barry. Madeline and I are quite frank in our discussions."

I spluttered, and if I hadn't been almost dehydrated by the stifling heat I probably would have spit right in his face. "Not in front of perfect strangers we aren't!"

"Barry's not a stranger, Madeline. He's my fiancé. Well—my almost fiancé—and it would help if you got used to it. Maybe he could offer some advice if you bothered to listen."

Barry's chest puffed up, I swear it did. "Madeline, if it's any help—"

"It won't be. Thank you all the same."

He grinned. "I wonder if you two realize how alike you are." Before I could argue Barry rushed on. "I just wanted to say that . . . well . . . I've had some experience with this kind of thing. . . . "

I rolled my eyes. "Do tell."

"Hee-hee-he . . ."

Wonder of wonders! Was that my mother giggling? Then I remembered what she and Barry had been up to since we'd arrived. "On second thought—*don't* tell! I've only just eaten."

"Now, Madeline," Barry continued, ignoring my choking sounds *and* the make-believe noose I tied around my neck, *and* the fact that I was tying it *very* tightly! "I've been there. I know things and I can tell you that boys, that is, guys, don't usually respect a girl who goes all out on the first date."

I gave the noose a final yank. "Oh, puleese. Just shoot me." My mouth flopped open and I just barely stopped my head from clunking against the wall. This was his idea of help?

Even Mom was looking at him like he'd dropped a cog. This was waay too amazing. This rated as Ripley's Believe It or Not stuff. Did the guy really think this was a news flash? I pitied his poor kids if they had to wait till nearly sixteen to get the lowdown on dating practices. Poor Barry—he was looking so . . . so . . . earnest. So . . . clueless. Call me the devil's spawn, but I simply could not let this opportunity pass. I put on my most innocent face. Too easy. "Is this the truth, Barry? You're kidding? Really? Oh, no!" I let myself fall onto the bed, the total picture of stricken misery. "Why didn't someone tell me before this? All those guys! All that lack of respect! I've been chalking it up in truckloads. Mom, why didn't you say something? I'll never be able to go home ever again! And here I thought everyone loved me for my impeccable sense of style. . . ."

I peeked out from between fingers splayed across my eyes. Barry's chest had sunk back to its usual unimpressive size. Maybe it had even caved a little. And was turning purple fatal? One could only hope. "Frances! Good heavens! Look at the child. I had no idea . . . we have to—"

Mom had gone back to the repacking. "She's okay Barry."

"Okay? *Okay!* How can you say that?" His voice was incredulous, his eyes looked like they were going to pop, and he just stared at Mom like he was seeing a stranger. This could only be good. "I can't believe you'd let her . . . Um I mean . . . she needs help. She needs couns—"

"She needs grounding," Mom finished dryly. "Get up, Madeline. I need to sort toiletries."

Game over. And just when Barry was having second thoughts. I rolled off the bed. My work here was unfinished—but I'd made a start.

Barry still wasn't sure, and he was swallowing so hard his weird little Adam's apple was jumping up and down like a Ping-Pong ball in a lottery machine. I still could not see what my mother saw in this man. His voice was shaky. "You mean she was . . . that she hasn't . . . ? That she already knew . . . ?"

I shrugged at him. "Fifth grade, Barry boy. Mrs. Lyons. Interpersonal Relationships class."

He didn't seem convinced. "Madeline, are you sure? I mean, if you find it difficult to talk to your mum . . . I guess it's just that you seemed so genuine."

My grin was smug. "Drama class. Straight As all the way."

He sagged a bit and I almost felt sorry for him. Almost.

Mom sighed. "You could apologize."

I was stunned. Apologize? Me? Could life possibly be more unfair than it already was? "Are you kidding? Why should I say 'sorry' to either of you when from the moment this trip started it's been one disaster after another? I've had everything personal and private—from

67

my underwear to hair removal wax to ultra-private-never-before-disclosed facts about my anatomy—all paraded in public! Like, hello, Mom! I don't have one secret left. No one seems to care that I've been totally humiliated more than once! Barry even knows about my sex life!"

"You don't have a sex life."

"Like that makes it better!"

She patted my cheek. "To me it does, sweetheart. . . ."

It was my turn to sag. Defeated, I flopped back on the bed again and this yucky watery stuff ran down between my shoulder blades. I refused to call it sweat. I have never made sweat in my life and I wasn't going to start now. "Are you really going to leave me here?" My voice was low and whiny. And it wasn't an act.

"It's just for a day or so, I promise." Then she gave me a hug. "We'll start off in the morning while it's still dark—it'll be cooler. But we'll be back as soon as we can."

It was happening—she really was leaving me here. I jammed back that darned lump that continued to clog up my throat and forced my voice to be firm. "I have no choice, do I? You and Barry get to leave this place. But me? I am a prisoner of Area Fifty-one, where I have to babysit the Brat and hope no aliens swoop down in their dinky little spaceship and suck out all my reproductive organs before you get back!" I spun on the bed. "I ask you honestly, Mom: Was this the future you dreamed for me when you gave birth?"

Mom finally closed the last case. Her hair hung limp around her face, which looked like someone had slicked oil all across it, and her shirt clung to her in big wet patches. All I could think was, ohmigod—did I look that bad? She blew at a strand of hair that flopped across her eyes and looked thoughtful. "Is this what I dreamed for you? Nooo, but in my dreams I skipped over your teenage years. I jumped straight from grade school to college graduation. So technically, in my dreams, this part doesn't exist. I found it easier that way."

"Very droll, Mother." I rolled off the bed.

Barry put his hand on my shoulder. He looked like he'd forgiven me. Drat. All that energy wasted. "Madeline, can you keep an eye on Jason? He'll be okay, but since his mum died . . . well, he can sometimes get nervous when we're apart. He'd never let on though. . . ."

The Brat would be shaky about his dad leaving? That bit was nearly my undoing. Not that I was ready to let everyone see that. I toughed it out again. "Is there anything I should, like, know?" I knew some of the details, but a recap probably wouldn't hurt. "She died in an accident, right?"

Barry nodded. "Jace was with her—but he wasn't hurt. He saw her bundled into an ambulance and never saw her alive again. He was seven."

Sheesh! Seven years old . . . My heart scrunched like a ball of wadded paper. That was a total bummer. In one of those little photographic flashes that scream across your brain I saw both our situations. The Brat won. Not knowing a parent was way easier than losing one you loved. Okay, so what was I supposed to say now? I went with a nod.

Barry looked like he was going to hug me, but I stepped away; I was back in control. "Well, considering nothing will change your mind about going, I'm taking a shower. Maybe that will help."

It was the look on Barry's face that halted my trek across the faded linoleum flooring. "Umm . . ." He shot a quick look at Mom.

"Honey, I think you should wait till tomorrow for your shower."

"But Mom, I'm filthy! I can taste this dust stuff right down my throat! It's clogging my eyelashes together, and my pores are screaming for help!"

She came across and patted my shoulder. "Trust me on this one. I think you've had enough sho—er, surprises for one day, and given your preoccupation with plumbing, maybe you should wait."

My heart sank. Oh, God. How bad could it be? Worse than the green chamber of secret horrors back at Barry's place? Surely not. But what if it was? Suddenly I was tired. Very tired. "My teeth?"

"Use the kitchen sink," Barry said. "We're going to."

Mom shoved a bag at me and I walked robotically toward the kitchen. "How disgusting. I am about to spit tooth germs where people prepare food."

In the hall I ran into the Brat. I couldn't see Mitch anywhere. Or his dad. Where did these people go to, anyway? I couldn't get past the sneaking suspicion that they had this really cool house somewhere up the road that had air-conditioning and an ice maker and a pool and three whole bathrooms. I mean, it was really hard to believe that people could live without indoor plumbing!

Or maybe Mitch had realized that he'd just lost the opportunity of a lifetime to find his one true love and had gone off to get his head straight and work out how to get me back.

Like I'd go back.

The Brat didn't look any more comfortable than I did. His clothes were sticking to him, and I was sure he felt just as dirty and gross as I did. I felt oddly protective toward him after my conversation with Barry, but I guess it didn't show. "Where are you going?" I asked.

"If it's any of your business, Miss New York Up Yourself, I'm going to see Dad."

I shrugged. So much for feeling sorry for him. "As if I care anyway. I'm going to find out which bedroom is mine."

I didn't like the smile he sent in my direction. Despite what I now knew, I still hadn't forgiven him for the cockroaches. Even after Barry explained they were really only candy covered dates, I still could *not* get that feeling of eating an insect out of my head. So, okay, I admit his smile made me nervous—but, hey, it wasn't like I didn't have good reason! And if I was snarky, then it was his own fault.

"Your bedroom?" he asked sweetly. Too sweetly.

Would there ever be any good news "Just spill it. You're dying to torture me. Might as well get your jollies while you can."

The smile was now a leer that threatened to be a laugh. "We're sleeping out in the lean-to. You're gonna love it. It even has air-conditioning!"

"Air-conditioning?" I almost kissed the kid and caught myself just in time. This heat was obviously making me delirious! Then his words hurtled back at me like a swinging demolition ball. "Did you say *we're* sleeping in this . . . what did you call it? Like you and me? We're sleeping *together*? In the same *bed*?"

My heart was threatening to explode. How disgusting! How revolting! How unhygienic! Ohmigod! How many times could I face death in one day?

The only thing that saved my mind from having a total meltdown was that the Brat was bent over in front of me pretending to barf. "Oh, grosseroo! Not *together,* you moron! I'd rather sleep over in the river with the crocodiles or out back with the goannas."

"Goannas? No—don't tell me. I don't want to know what they are. I'm focusing only on the bed situation—I take it you meant there are two beds?"

"Do you think I'd be sleeping there if there weren't?"

"Well, that's better than nothing. I'm so tired. . . . I'm going to climb into bed and e-mail home."

This time the kid totally broke up. "Haven't you worked it all out yet? There aren't any lines out here! No phone! No Internet. No e-mail! No texting . . . This is the Outback, Madeline!"

No e-mail! No texting? I felt my heart start to close off blood supply to the rest of my body. No e-mail? I was shut off from the world! Isolated!

Barry poked his head out the door—when he saw me his face lit up. "Oh, Madeline, I thought of some more advice. Play hard to get. It works every time."

I couldn't answer; I turned and walked away. Not only was I still in shock, I could *not* take dating advice from a man wearing lime satin boxer shorts covered in pulsating purple hearts that spouted red salivating tongues. My mother was on the road to self-destruction. How could she live with herself? How could that be her last sight before trying to sleep? Didn't the woman have nightmares?

Spinning back just once, the assault on my fashion sense wasn't quite the earthquake it had been the first time. Probably because my head was still reeling from my electronics denial—still, I avoided the view as best I could. "Hey, Brat?" I asked in a still-shaky voice. "Where's this den of luxury we're sharing?"

He looked innocent. "The lean-to? It's at the end of the house. Second door off the kitchen on the left."

Brushing my teeth and taking care not to swallow any water that might later demand to be released, I thought about his words. Lean-to? These country people were just too precious. Despite my recent shocks I had almost gone beyond caring. It suddenly didn't matter what it was called as long as it had a nice comfy bed with crisp, pure cotton sheets and delicious air-con. Pity I had to share. Or did I? As I got closer to the room I was already thinking of as total heaven, the evil twin who lived inside me was waaaay ahead of the kid. I'd just get there first and lock him out. Too easy.

Then I got there.

And all my thoughts turned to hell and how to make a certain Brat pay. Big-time!

My wail was drowned out by his laughter. He'd sneaked in behind me. "What's the matter? I thought you wanted air-conditioning. You can't get better than this."

"Better than what? There are no walls! This is a porch with a roof! A porch that's falling down!" Suddenly I knew why it was called a lean-to. The place was collapsing, and I would be crushed under rotting timber and rusty iron. And I was probably overdue for my tetanus shot. I threw myself down on one of the two camp beds I could just make out from the light sneaking in from the kitchen and buried my face in my hands. My friends back home would never believe the tortures I'd been through. "This isn't even Hicksville. This is Hicksville to the max. This place is too primitive even for hicks! Hicks wouldn't come here. . . ."

Then I stilled. I heard the Brat flop onto the other bed. "Jason? What was that you said about crocodiles in the river? Like, is there a river close by? And is there a fence around it? A crocodile-safe fence?"

My answer was a fake snore.

Great. Well, that was the last time I'd be nice to him! I rolled over and tried to forget that whatever I was lying on was prickling me and that every bug known to man was eating me alive. I smacked at two more. Why worry about crocodiles? The mosquitoes promised to suck me dry. There'd be nothing left but a skeleton in the morning.

Between the heat and the bugs I never imagined I'd sleep a wink—but I did. At first I wasn't sure what woke me. It was still black outside, and my first sensation was that a breeze had come up and it was quite cool! Yay!

The second thing I noticed was the stars. They really were beautiful. Like diamonds on a black velvet display cloth. Of course, nothing could ever replace the real thing, and Tiffany's would always win out. But it was a pretty good imitation. If you were into imitations . . .

I stretched. Then I noted the third thing. The noise. It was obviously what had woken me. It was kind of a grunting. And something else . . . Did crocodiles grunt? My heart stopped again, and I wondered how much of this stop/start stuff it was going to take. Lying very still, I closed my eyes and tried to follow the source and direction of the noise.

When I eventually did, my whole stomach rose into my mouth. Even in this light I could make out the insidious movement. It was awful. . . . The most horrid thing. Oh, God—I would simply never recover from this. Ever.

I tossed the sheet aside and my scream pierced the night. . . .

Chapter Five

Jason jerked into a sitting position. By now my eyes were adjusted to the dark and I could make things out very clearly. Too clearly!

"What the—"

"Th-this place is a horror farm! Quick! Get it! Kill it! D-disgusting, slimy, wild animals! H-huge! Uggghhhhh! It was on me! *On me!* On my person! Uggghhhhhhh!"

A band of light fell across our beds. "What's going on, guys?"

"I dunno, Mitch. She's loony! She just started screaming. She's gonna wake everyone!"

"No one to wake but us, mate. They left earlier—try to avoid the rain up the track a bit."

My heart thumped harder; my mother wasn't even here to defend me? Great!

I was standing upright on my camp bed now, shuddering. I would have crawled up the wall to get away from this totally disgusting beastie if I could have. "Eoww! The images are just too gross! I'm going to be scarred for life! I will *never* get over this. *Never*! It was soo ugly!"

The Brat's voice sounded confused. Like he was confused! He knew exactly what I meant. "What are you talking about?"

Mitch's laughter stopped us both, and I finally turned to him. Big mistake. The bottom half of him was in shadow but the top half was totally naked. Oh, my. Really nice chest . . . Muscles. Tanned. I slipped a peek lower and inhaled too quickly and almost choked for real. I couldn't see clothes! Any clothes!

Diving back onto the bed headfirst, I shoved my head into the pillow.

"Now what's with her?" the Brat whined.

I pointed to where I thought the Brat sat. "You have no right to whine. You aren't the injured party here. And you?" This time my finger went to where I hoped Mitch was standing. "I refuse to talk to any guy who is naked!"

His gravelly voice reached out to me. "Lucky I'm wearing jocks then. Or then again, if it means you're gonna start yapping, maybe I'm not so lucky. . . ."

The Brat laughed. Typical.

I pulled the pillow down a teeny bit. "Are you sure?"

"Jeez, Madeline, who cares! It's a hundred and twenty degrees out here!"

I turned on the Brat. "That's just the attitude I'd expect

77

from someone like you. Someone who . . . who'd put a huge, hideous goanna frog on another person's bed. I could be covered in warts tomorrow!"

"Who *what*?"

Mitch grinned at the Brat. "I think Madeline had a visit from one of our famous cane toads." To me he added, "A goanna is a lizard, Madeline. A really large one. A lot like an iguana. I think what you saw was a toad."

"Toad, frog—who cares! I'm being terrorized here! This was no random visit, Mitch—I caught some movement just before I locked eyes with that thing. That Brat's been trying to get at me since I arrived—he put it there on purpose!"

"I wha . . . ?" Okay, I couldn't see the Brat's face go red but I did hear him stutter. "No! I didn't! Jeez! Cane toads are nasty things—I wouldn't go near one in a million years! Not even to get at you, Miss Up Yourself! Jeez!"

Mitch's voice was gentle. Kind. *Kind?!* "Don't worry."

"Don't worry? Aaaak! Wrong! I think he should worry! Worry *a lot* because when I get over this and get hold of him—"

Mitch ignored me and spoke to the Brat. "It's okay, mate."

To me he said, "Madeline, Jace is right. No one would touch a cane toad—they can be poisonous. He'd never do that—that critter got here all on his own steam. Came up out of the river 'cause it's dry. We haven't had many—but I should have thought of that."

Darn it all—but Mitch made sense. Still, I wasn't prepared to give up. "But I saw him moving!"

"It was mozzie bites," the Brat yelled. "They're itching like crazy." He stuck his leg out. I couldn't see anything, but it didn't stop his pointing to some supposed lumps on his leg. As if!

The Brat flopped back on his bed with a big sigh that sounded just like a sulky tantrum. Personally that was the least of my problems! "Well aren't you at least going to go and find this poisonous thing and kill it? Or cripple it so it can't come after me again?"

Mitch finally turned to me, pointing into the pitch black nothingness just an arm's length away. "Got any ideas where to look?" He shook his head. "Madeline—this is wild country, we're the intruders—not the wildlife. You can't go chasing down everything that's poisonous around here—you'd never get to do anything else." His voice softened. "You were just unlucky, most times they stay out of our way."

"And this is supposed to make me feel better?" My voice wobbled as I spoke and I hated that fact!

I think Mitch noticed but he didn't say anything about it. Thank goodness. There was this big, long silence and when he did speak his own voice was gentle and low, like he was trying to make it up to me. "Madeline? I, um, I was thinking . . . I probably just should have come out and asked before. . . . Um, I don't suppose you'd like to sleep in my bed?"

What? His bed? Any screaming, *aaac*king and wob-

79

bling stopped instantly. *Sleep in his bed?* Where had that come from? Oh, what I would have given at that moment for a tape recorder or a videocamera. My friends at home would never believe this. Of course, I had no intention of saying yes—but it did my girlie heart good to hear him say he had finally realized that he couldn't live without me. Call it my too-soft nature, but I'd forgiven him again. How could you stay mad at a guy as sweet as that?

"Dad and I should have thought of it earlier," he continued.

I swallowed deeply. "Your dad would approve?"

"Sure! Mum would have insisted, but Dad and I are a bit clueless about all this stuff."

Eeeooww. "Your mom would have insisted?" Now that was just plain sick. How did something so charming turn into something so creepy in just a few words? Maybe I should have looked a bit more closely at the family pedigree before giving my heart so easily. Had I just fallen into the swampy end of the gene pool? *Double eeeowww.* Those kinds of nasty surprises I could live without. If I wanted firsthand experience of a freak show I only had to look at Barry and the Brat.

"Mum? Yeah. She'll clip me around the ears for not thinking to swap with you straight off."

I stared at him, speechless. Finally I found my voice. "Swap? Oh, *swap.*" Okay—I could cope. "Swapping is good." Yes, swapping *was* good. Swapping meant there were no loonies in the family.

But had swapping meant that he hadn't just asked me to . . . ?

So how did that stand with how he felt about me? And what about how I felt about him? Was he still forgiven?

"Come on. I'll just show you the room and grab my pillow and we can all get back to sleep. You guys have had a big day."

As I followed him into his room I had my answer: the guy was giving up his bed for me. Not just a seat on the subway or first dibs on a cab or some of his fries. He'd given up his bed.

I couldn't think of anything more romantic.

I lay there and soaked up the warmth of where his body had lain. Even in this heat it was a very cool thing to feel. His room had these doors that opened onto another porch, and a great breeze was coming in straight at me. But it didn't hide his smell. That great outdoorsy smell just wound itself around me. Heaven . . .

From out back I heard the mumble of voices. The Brat's was first. I lay very still and concentrated. He sounded really upset and I suddenly felt mean. "I know you said it's okay and everything, Mitch, but I swear I didn't do it. . . ."

I heard the smile in Mitch's voice. "It's okay, mate; I believe you. I'm the one who lives here, remember? I know how it works out here. I know you wouldn't have touched a cane toad."

"Really?"

"Fair dinkum. No sweat. And don't worry about

Madeline. She's kinda not like ordinary people. . . . Not like us . . ."

I waited. Did that mean he thought I was special?

He went on. "She's a bit of a princess, if you know what I mean."

I heard the Brat chuckle. Mitch had made him feel better—but I'd been the one who made him feel bad in the first place. My stomach twisted and I felt that lump move into my throat, but I pushed it back again.

I swallowed hard and pulled my lips into a tight line I never cried, and I wasn't going to start now. Besides, it would probably only lead to more dehydration, and I didn't even dare think about what that salt would do to the skin around my eyes!

Instead I went back over Mitch's words. I was a princess? That's how Mitch saw me? Okay—so I was different; I knew that. I was used to different things, a different way of life. To be honest it nagged at me a bit, and when I finally fell asleep I wasn't dreaming about royal weddings and Mitch and me decked out in the royal carriage with crowds waving at us from the sidewalk.

And considering how my mind usually works, that bothered me.

When I woke up I was even more bothered. Mom had already left and I needed to pee again. Badly. So much for not letting any liquid pass my lips! To think I risked wrinkles for this and it didn't even work!

As I crept out through the kitchen the guys were there eating breakfast. "Afternoon," Mitch said as I tried not to let on about my problem. The Brat chuckled. Again. Oh, my—weren't these two palsy-walsy all of a sudden.

And to think last night I'd actually been feeling sorry for the Brat!

I looked across at them. Big mistake. I wasn't fooling anyone. Mitch's eyes were twinkling, and I had to look away really fast. The gooey stuff he did to my stomach was not good for trying to control a bladder!

On the porch, I stared at the toilet sitting way over in the middle of long, scrappy grass. Long grass that was probably full of deadly snakes just waiting to jump up and swallow me whole. I gulped and felt my bladder tighten a bit more. . . . Maybe there were crocodiles.

Call me a coward, but I just couldn't do it. I had to head back behind the shed. Back inside the kitchen, neither of them looked my way. But they knew. Drat them.

Mitch's eyes were still dancing when he asked me if I wanted any breakfast. "I can do you bacon and eggs. We just had some."

Pulling out a chair, I looked at their greasy plates and nearly barfed. "No, I'll just have some muesli and yogurt with a banana, thank you."

It was the silence that made me look up. Mitch's smile was different now—kind of like I was this simple little kid he had to be patient with. *Pfft!* As if. "Would corn flakes and powdered milk and canned peaches do?"

"Oh." Of course—I should have thought. These were the people who didn't go to the spa and thought department stores were like some natural wonder you went to look at once a year on your vacation! Like the Grand Canyon, for crying out loud!!! So why would they have anything decent for breakfast? I tried to calm down, but it was harder than I imagined. "A hot roll?"

"Toast?" he offered back.

I nodded. "Coffee?"

"Tea."

Toast and tea? Toast and tea. I could cope.

Mitch hopped up to get it ready, and I *was* going to help—really—but my head had just started to pound like someone was inside with a jackhammer. He turned and looked at me. "You okay?"

"Yeah. I think I just need some asprin. I'll just go and—"

He was right beside me before I'd barely moved. His hands dropped onto my shoulders and pushed me back into the chair. "I think you need water, mate. The only way to cope with this heat is to drink heaps of water." Almost before I realized he'd left me he was back with a glass of cold water, which he pressed into my hands. "Drink this, Maddie." His voice was all soft and rumbly. "Then I'll get you another one."

He kind of held his hands around mine when he pushed the glass into them. I opened my mouth to tell him I was Madeline—that no one *ever* called me Maddie. *Ever.* But I couldn't say the words. All I could do was stare at his smooth, tanned skin. His hands were soft; I hadn't expected that. His face was smooth like that too, and I wondered if it was as soft. . . .

And so I drank. And prayed that my bladder suddenly found new and greater depths of capacity. . . .

I came out of my daze to hear him asking me if I wanted to try some Vegemite.

"Oh. Okay—Vegemite. I've heard of that—you Aussies eat a lot of this stuff, don't you?" See? I could play Miss Perfect Guest if I wanted to. "What's it like?"

Mitch passed some over. "Work it out yourself."

It was in a jar. It was black and it was smelly. "Oh, kind of like caviar? But smooth? I love caviar!"

I scooped out a huge splodge of it and went to spread it on the toast, but again Mitch's hand grabbed mine. "Hey! Way too much!"

Too much? Ohmigod, had I just been, like . . . like, a pig or something? Was this their only ration till, like, next Christmas? But he was laughing—so he couldn't have been too mad. Personally I thought he just liked holding my hand the first time and was looking for another excuse.

Maybe I would have even believed that if the Brat hadn't banged his fist on the table then. "Oh, man!" he whined. "Why did you stop her? That would have been awesome! Talk about a major puke!"

"What? What did I do?"

Mitch was still laughing. "Just go easy at first. It's really strong, kind of an acquired taste. And no, it's nothing like caviar—well, I don't think it is. I've never actually had caviar. This is a yeast extract—it's kind of salty. We don't layer it on—we just kind of smear it."

"Oh." It was good advice, and I hardly choked at all. Of course, if Mitch hadn't stopped me it would have been a different thing entirely. Still, it would have been him and the Brat wearing it when I spewed—not me. All that aside, the stuff wasn't as bad as I expected. Okay, it wasn't caviar—but then again, I'd chucked my caviar the first time I had that too. Not that I ever admitted that to anyone.

I was learning fast that Mitch was a nice guy. Not just hot—but nice.

Another thing I knew for sure was that he was no doctor. A gallon of water later my headache was no better. Maybe a shower would fix it. I was just going to ask where it was when a roar and splatter of dust turned us all to the doorway.

The motorbike was switched off and this person walked into the house. Straight in—without knocking! But like that was a worry! It wasn't like they ever closed doors around this place.

It was a girl person. I knew that because it had breasts—but otherwise I'd have still been guessing. She had on jeans that no designer would dare put his name on, boots, and this really, really ugly Guns N' Roses T-shirt. Like, what century was this girl living in?

Then she took her helmet off and this thick dark brown hair fell out. And she had on no makeup! Not one slash of mascara—not one dab of lip gloss! Nothing! Why? Was it because of the heat? I was amazed. All in all she had good bone structure. Nice eyes. Pretty face.

I figured she was about fourteen. Great potential, actually—the makeover guys would love her. Made-up she'd be stunning. . . .

If my friend Sabrina had been here this girl wouldn't stand a chance. Sabrina would have had her stripped, colored, styled, and made-up in less time than it took to say, "Frappuccino." Sabrina had a makeover fetish. No one is allowed to be undone; everyone has to be model-perfect all the time.

On second thought, maybe this girl was better off.

"Hey, Cal! How's it going?" Then Mitch turned to us. "This is Madeline and that's Jason. They're staying with us for a few days. Guys? This is Calliopie. We just call her Callie."

Callie smiled. Nice teeth. "Gidday. Youse are the Americans, are ya? Never met an American." Her voice was soft and drawly.

Mitch laughed. "Not Jason. He's an Aussie like us—but a city slicker. Madeline's the Yank. New York." To us Mitch said, "Cal lives down the road. It's her house you can just see down at the bottom of the paddock."

Well, that explained a lot. Callie obviously didn't get out much. "Paddock?" I put out my hand to shake hers. "Hi, Callie, great to meet you, too."

"Hi, Maddie—nice to meet you." She laughed. "A paddock? Maybe you'd call it a field? Dunno. It's just like a big bit of fenced-in land that we run the animals on. You know, the horses or cattle or sheep. Most of these properties are divided into paddocks."

The more she smiled, the more I realized she was just shy. Well, she could rest easy; I wasn't going to bite. Besides, it'd be nice to have another girl around. Even if she wasn't exactly a fashionista. I sighed—a mere few days would never be enough for me to impart everything I knew. I'd just have to do my best. It was the least I could do for a fellow sister. And even if I *was* suffering the most excruciating pain anyone has ever suffered in the history of woman. Man! I had to get rid of this headache!

She handed Mitch something. "Dad's fixed the radio. Oh, and he said to tell you he's taken the dogs out to the west quarter."

Mitch nodded. "No sweat. And tell him thanks for the radio—I'll hook it up in a tick."

Fascinating as this conversation was, I was getting desperate. "Mitch, could you show me the bathroom, please? I'd like to take a nice hot shower."

I saw them all look at each other—but I was ready this time. "I saw that look." I put my hands up to calm them. "Okay, I'm not afraid. I am not. I've been warned and I've already figured that this is another version of the green chamber and so I can cope. Okay?" Then I stalled. "Ohmigod. As long as it's not chartreuse. It's not chartreuse, is it? Chartreuse would be the end."

This time everyone stared at me. Had I really said that? Okay—I'd had a pineapple moment. A totally "out there" moment, and yes, I felt like an idiot. But could anybody blame me?

It was the heat. Had to be . . .

Finally Mitch spoke. "Um, yeah. This way."

My eyes got wider as they followed his direction. My heart rate got faster.

That way?

No! Not *that* way!

He was going outside! No! There was a kitchen with running water! Why not a bathroom? It wasn't much to ask! It wasn't a big jump.

He kept going. . . . Puleese, not that way!

My eye twitched but I ignored it. It had to be the headache. It could not be that I was going rapidly insane. The bathroom could *not* be outside. It could not!

Waaah! It was! And I even stooped so low as to wish it *had* been chartreuse. My friends and I had sworn off chartreuse since *Vogue* said it was the most totally out color for summer. But even chartreuse would be better than this!

It wasn't even a room. I just stared. It was this huge burlap potato bag draped around four poles to make a square shower-stall shape. It stood on a wooden stage-type thing and above it, taped to one of the poles with black duct tape, was this shower-spray nozzle.

Ohmigod, I mouthed. No sound would come out.

"Um, if you just get your things I'll hook the pump up." That was Mitch, but his voice sounded a looong way away. "Cal? Will you get Maddie a towel?"

I felt her move. But I was frozen to the spot. I could not . . . I would not . . .

But I had no choice.

When I returned with my bath pack and a towel wrapped around me, I stepped up onto that platform. Still dazed, I could only think of those people who'd been beheaded in France all those gazillion years ago. The time when that lady—Madame de Faberge or something—knitted while the heads rolled. I knew how they'd all felt. I held my head tall and proud.

Everyone was staring at me. "Ohmigod—I feel like I'm going to the guillotine. I'm just going to say this one thing: If any one of you pulls out a cross-stitch or paint-by-numbers you will be very sorry."

"What? She's a loony."

Mitch chuckled. "Yeah, mate—but she's an original. . . ."

I turned to my new best friend. "Callie?"

As expected she bounded onto the platform, and I graciously let her take my towel. There I stood in all my glory in my brand-new bikini for all to admire. Well, actually for Mitch to admire. Okay—I admit that I wasn't, like, so dazed that I hadn't seen an opportunity coming! An innocent victim of inhumane torture I might be—but come on! I hadn't stopped breathing!

The purple and aqua really gave my skin that special glow; the triangles hugged my curves—what there was of them. And so what if there was a little bit of extra something sewn into the cups? It wasn't like it was a crime, for crying out loud! I couldn't be arrested for it! The plan was for it to take attention away from the fact that the rest of me looked a bit scrawny. Okay, so I didn't have that undernourished-catwalk-model look, but a couple of pounds wouldn't hurt.

Not once would I let on that it mattered, though. That was what Mom had always taught me: Look and act confident and people believe you are. I flicked a quick glance in Mitch's direction to make sure it was working, and he was totally besotted. He was. Good. *See it and weep, buster.*

Then, with a little swirl, I stepped behind the potato-sack curtain. And turned the handle.

Chapter Six

The rest followed in, like, kind of slow motion. I looked up toward the shower and saw the drops push through the little holes in the nozzle and slowly make their way to me. To the side of me voices carried like those really creepy computer voices they use in scary movies. . . .

"Did you tell her?"

"Nah. Did you?"

"Me either . . ."

"Tell me what?" What did I care? The water was warm; I needed this so badly. I turned my face to the spray, opened my mouth. . . . "Eowww! Ahhhh! Ohmigod! Yuck! Spffft! Pffft! This is disgusting. This is like—Ohmigod—this is like a gazillion dogs suddenly farted in here! Get me out!" This was filth! This was worse than the worst gym socks! "I can't breathe! I'm being poisoned!" Diving out of that stinky little shower, I skidded on the wet wooden platform. *Ouch! Damn!*

Splinter! "What is it with you people? Is there one thing in this country that doesn't bite, sting, scratch, or stink?"

The Brat screwed up his face. "Is that . . . ?"

"Rotten-egg gas. Yep."

Spitting as much of the disgusting stuff as I could from my mouth, I stared at Mitch. "You put rotten eggs in the shower with me?"

Callie came up with the towel. "It's the minerals in the bore water, Maddie. That's what makes it smell that bad."

"What is it with this 'Maddie' stuff!?" I snatched at the towel and tried to wipe the inside of my mouth. I stopped after the sixth gag. "I cannot believe this is happening. How do I get this totally gross stuff off me?"

I heard Mitch and the Brat chuckle. So did my used-to-be new best friend, Callie. Big, big mistake. "You have to get back in, Maddie. And use some shampoo."

If she said "Maddie" one more time I would . . . "I have to get back in? Are you crazy?"

"It's the only way. . . ."

"Well, I demand a full face mask! Or at least a nose plug! Something! Anything so that I don't have to inhale that smell! 'Cause if I do I am going to puke big-time, and I will not be the one cleaning it up!" So *what* if I was whiny! Dropping to a squat I wrapped my arms around my tummy. "This is so not funny. I have a foul headache, I'm gagging on rotten-egg gas, and now my tummy has started to cramp! I just want to know one thing: Since when has taking a shower become an event on *Fear Fac-*

tor? Next thing I know you'll be expecting me to eat live worms!"

The Brat was enjoying himself waaay too much. He would so pay for this. Callie wasn't. She looked a bit spooked. Well, what? Hadn't the girl ever seen anyone express a rational opinion before?

And where the heck was Mitch? I tried to remember whether I was talking to him and I couldn't. Had I forgiven him again—or had I taken it back? Sheesh—how was a girl supposed to keep score? It was like I was expected to do everything in this relationship, even remember if we were talking to each other!

His voice broke into my pity party. "Here. Try this. I was looking for my old snorkeling mask. Can't find it—but I found this. Had it since I was a kid. It's a bit old—just watch that elastic. Might be better than nothing."

"You think?" I could not keep the sarcasm out of my voice, and the absolute only reason I didn't thump my forehead against my knees was that it would have hurt. A lot. "You think a plastic clown nose will be better than nothing? Oh, puleese just shoot me!"

He didn't. Instead he plonked the elastic over my head and shoved the nose into place.

Eeeoww. What about nose germs? I pulled it down just a fraction. "Has anyone's nose but yours ever been in this?" The words came out all nasally.

He shook his head, but he couldn't hide the grin.

"You swear?"

"I swear."

I pushed it back into place and stood up and turned back to the shower. Okay—my second entrance was not going to be as grand as the first. Should I have been surprised? It was at that moment when I stood under that putrid shower in my beautiful new bikini and my red plastic clown nose that I recognized the truth: I really *was* allergic to Australia. Some people were allergic to pollen. I was allergic to a whole country. . . .

Callie was beside me again and handing over shampoo. "Wash your whole body with this, Maddie. Soap won't lather in bore water."

Maddie? I swear, my eyes crossed. "Thank you, *Calliopie*."

Duh! She didn't even notice! She smiled at me, for crying out loud!

Take two was in record time, hair and all (Mom would *not* have believed it!), and I swear my oral hygienist would have awarded me a trip to the Caribbean for how well I scrubbed my teeth, tongue, and gums afterward. The ever-present Callie was ever present. I was starting to feel like I was her science project! "Why doesn't this water in the kitchen taste as bad as that other stuff?"

"Tank water. We collect it when it rains and store it in big underground tanks."

"Haven't you people heard of pure, natural bottled water? You could save yourself sooo much trouble."

Finally, back in Mitch's room, I got to be alone for a minute and worked out what the cramps and headache were. No, not intestinal trouble brought on by the bathroom from hell. Worse—well, almost worse. The monthly miseries. Of course! I should have expected they'd come early. Why not? Everything that could have possibly gone wrong, had. Why not this too? Why should I be surprised to get my period in a place that required a ticket on a jumbo jet to purchase the nearest chocolate bar?

At least there was Midol.

I flopped onto the bed. In my entire life I had no idea misery could be this miserable. I even had to force myself to moisturize my face and cream my legs. I had never once in my whole life—well, since I was six—ever had to force myself to cream my legs. A little thought trickled in that I was always trying to make my mom proud of me— do what she would do—but I shoved it aside. I had bigger problems than psychoanalyzing my relationship with my mom.

This was bad.

I put on clean underwear and shorts and stuff but I left my bikini top on. The morning was getting later and the heat haze was already doing its shimmy and I just didn't think I could bear any more clothes on my body. It was a total steambath out there.

Callie arrived to see if she could help. Well, duh! With what?

"I'm fine. I'll just do my makeup and then let my hair dry free in the heat."

That's when disaster number 631 struck. I told myself

to stay calm. I told myself I was just confused. I told myself this could not be happening. . . .

But it was!

There was no mistake.

There was no makeup!

"Aaaack!" To say I totally wigged out was an understatement. I searched everywhere! But no makeup bag. Not even anything that looked like a makeup bag. And it's not like I could, like, lose it! It was hot purple and the size of a medium suitcase!

"This can't be happening! Everything I need to survive in the outside world is in that bag!"

"It's not that bad, Maddie. . . ."

"Not that bad! *Not that bad?* You have no idea! It's all gone: my privately mixed foundation with its SPF thirty-plus sunblock that was delicately blended to smooth over my face with such subtlety that you hardly knew it was there. My Break of Dawn blush. My high-calorie lash-fattening mascara. My tricolor pack of smoky blue-gray eye shadows with the six darkening shades to enhance my eyes as day moved to night. The subtle smoky eyeliner to widen and deepen. My vanilla-essence-extract perfume that the shop assistant at Barneys told me had been created with me in mind. Me! And the absolute worst of all . . . my Kiss Me and Taste the Wild Strawberries lip gloss. All missing without a trace . . . Sob . . ."

Callie was looking at me like I was speaking a foreign language. "But you're beautiful like you are."

"You don't understand! It's taken *months* of experimenting to finally achieve such a natural look. And now it's gone. . . ."

Oooooh! This was so unfair! The one time in my life when I needed to taste like wild strawberries more than at any other time, and what happens? It's not there! I ask you, was anyone in the entire world living a worse life than me? "I could go on *Oprah* with this! I could write a book! They'd make a movie!" I did take a moment to consider that my English grades may need just a teeny bit of improvement before I wrote the book—but, hey, isn't that what ghostwriters are for?

On trembling legs I lowered myself onto the bed. "Well, Callie, there's really only one course of action open to me. I'm going to have to inhabit the dark world, a world where people move in shadows and hide from light. Move over, Buffy—here I come. . . ."

"The dark world?"

"Yes. And by the way, I don't suppose you know how one becomes a vampire? Short answers only—I don't have much time."

Of course she didn't. Sheesh, that girl had to get out more. Of course, she didn't understand my distress either. She dragged me to the kitchen where to my absolute horror she actually asked Mitch and the Brat what they thought of my naked facial state.

Oh, puleese stop the torture!

"Hate that gunk." That was the Brat—but, like, what did he know?

Mitch's reaction was different. He was fiddling with the radio Callie had given him earlier (great—maybe we'd at least get some decent music now!), and he stopped and looked up. And kept looking . . . Then he smiled that slow, lazy smile. "I like it better."

That smile . . . "B-better?"

The smile got deeper. This time I wasn't imagining anything. I really did know it was for me. "Yeah—better."

I couldn't help the smile I sent back. Maybe these strong, silent types weren't so bad. I'd never known a guy to say so much in so few words.

If this was a movie, the music would have swelled at that moment. Instead this nasally kind of voice appeared from nowhere: "Are ya there, Mitch, or not? Where are ya? Gone walkabout? The lady here wants to check on the kids."

Mitch spun back to the radio and pressed a little lever.

Ohmigod—this was their telephone! I did the whole eye-roll thing. "So much for killing our romantic moment," I was careful just to mutter. I didn't want to scare him off now that we'd gotten this far.

Mitch spoke into the radio. "Sorry, Dad. Yeah, I'm here. Fire away."

It was his dad? Stan? "Hey, is that my mom? Is she there too?"

"Ay, Dad? Is Frances there? Maddie wants to talk to her."

He got out of his seat and I took his place. "Just press this little lever when you want to speak and let it go when you've finished. Okay? It'll take a minute for them to answer you. And there's just one other th—"

"Madeline? Is that you?"

"Shoosh, Mitch!" I pressed the lever. "Mom?"

"But . . ." Sheesh! He was trying again!

Hello! Could the guy not take a hint? First he was strong and silent, and then he wouldn't shut up when I needed to talk to my mom! "Shush!"

I saw him throw his hands in the air, and then he went out on the porch. The Brat went too. No prizes for guessing what Callie did. Great. But at least I had *some* privacy. "Mom? I'm here! Have you got the thing for the car? Are you on your way back?"

"Not quite, honey. Barry and I have just discovered it's what they call the wet season right now, and some of the crossings are blocked. We've had to take some detours and it's made us real slow. We're about an hour or two out of Darwin now."

This was not what I wanted to hear. "Oh."

"Madeline? Are you okay? Is Jason okay?"

I felt the lump move to my throat again, but I pushed it back. "Sure, Mom. The Brat is okay. And me? Well, I won't even go into the whole shower disaster! But sure, I *could* be okay if I had my makeup! Mom? Did you take my makeup?"

There was a crackle and then she said, "I'm sorry, honey. In the dark, Barry picked that bag up as well."

I let my head drop onto the counter as I depressed the lever. "You know, the evidence is mounting, Mom. No court would argue when I have you declared insane. The guy is a loser! L-O-S-E-R!"

"What did you say? I lost you. . . ."

I sighed. "The point is, I am totally miserable, Mom! I am in torture here. The pain won't stop! I simply cannot use that toilet, and to make matters worse, now I have to suffer the rapid ruby rush. Early! Like, tell me *that's* fair!"

"Ruby . . . ? Oh, you have your period? Do you have everything you need?"

"Like, what do *you* think? Unless you've left a secret stash of Mars bars, then sorry, Mom—no, I don't think so."

"You have tampons? Midol?"

"Yea . . . Aaack!" My heart stopped (again). "Mom! My Midol was in my makeup bag! Oh, God—no chocolate! And no pain relief either? How could you do this to me, Mom? I will not survive. I swear, Mom, I mean it this time. I will *not* survive."

"Honey, you're breaking up and I'm going to have to hang up. You'll survive, but I'll bring chocolate back with me. Okay? See you, honey. Take care of Jason."

She was gone. I sat and stared at the radio, which was still crackling—but she'd stopped talking. I felt my bottom lip start to quiver, but I bit down on it. I was Madeline Frances Flannagan. I was a survivor. I was a chip off the old block. I was tough.

I was about to get up when the radio crackled again. She was back? I started to smile but it froze midway.

"Yoo-hoo? Girlie over at Stan's place?"

"Whaaaa?"

"This is Elsie here from Wallaby Crossing, love. Couldn't help but hear your little problem. Us girls have got to stick together now, don't we? Ay? Try some brandy and port wine, love. Just a sip. Works every time for those cramps! Cheerio, now."

My eyes grew bigger. I dived from the chair, staring at the radio like it was alive; smacking at it. "Aaah! Stop! Stop!"

"If that doesn't work, lovey"—Ohmigod—there was another one—"then try some brandy warmed up with orange juice and brown sugar. Works a treat for me, love. It'll help with that little toilet problem too. Makes you go like clockwork, if you know what I mean. . . . Tootlepip and good luck from May over at Alcheringa."

My mouth was dry. My eyes were glazed. My mouth spat out little sounds like warning squeaks from a dying battery in a smoke detector.

"Madeline, is it? Fay here, dearie. My daughters always swore by a good old-fashioned hot-water bottle. Don't you go listening to those others that want to fill you up with that demon alcohol. I'm at Coopers River if you need me. Just holler for Fay and I'll hear ya! Don't let that constipation get ahold, though, will you, love. That can be real nasty. And the gas it causes isn't pleasant for anyone else either, if you get my drift. Not the thing a young girl wants to put up with. Or anyone else, for that

102

matter. Brown sugar and hot water'll do it, dearie. 'Bye now."

My face was burning. I clutched at it, trying to hide, to crawl inside myself. "Who . . . ? Where . . . ?"

Before anyone else could speak, I dived on the lever and depressed it. Holding my nose, I tried to disguise my voice. "We can hold off on the advice now. Madeline has passed away. She's gone. Dead. Six feet under. You heard it here first. Madeline has left the building for the last time. Got it? So there is no need for any more advice. No more advice! No more. Ever. Got it?"

Callie was hiding her laughter behind her arm. Like I couldn't see that! "Oh, go ahead and laugh! It's such a great joke!"

She did. "They don't mean harm, Maddie. They're trying to help."

"It's *Madeline*! And I don't need their help! All I needed was chocolate and Midol! Now . . . now everyone knows my business. My really, really private business." My voice rose to a screech. "This is just, like . . . like, total humiliation—I've never been this humiliated. . . ."

Mitch came back in and the fire in my face turned into an inferno. Oh, God—he knew. There were probably speakerphones in the yard! "Ohmigod! The world knows! I'll be tomorrow's newspaper headline! I just know it! And why not? It isn't like anything *else* happens in this place. You people would never end up as a pro-

103

gram on the Lifestyle channel—because you have to *have* a lifestyle before that can happen!"

Mitch's mouth was not laughing, but his eyes gave him away. "That's what I was trying to tell you. It's a community band radio, Maddie—Madeline. Everyone hears what everyone else says. It keeps everyone safe— we all know if someone needs help. And I guess it's a bit of entertainment as well. We don't get TV out here."

That one stopped me for a moment. "No TV? Eee-owww." Then I remembered my humiliation. "Entertainment?! My life is a soap opera to these people?"

"Madeline? Georgia here, love . . . I've had a thought—"

"No! No! No!" I didn't wait to hear what Georgia had to say. I flew out the door. I didn't know where I was going, but I had to get away from everyone. And that darned radio.

Hitting the porch, I spun back at them. "And I am *not* constipated!"

"Maddie! Wait!"

"Maddie?"

I didn't wait but I did slow up a bit. I quickly discovered there was a problem with running away in the outback. Well, there was if you were afraid of everything that moved. And the way my luck was running, if it moved it was deadly and it was carrying a card with my name on it. Heck, there was probably a reward hanging over my head!

I stopped.

And Mitch was right there beside me.

He put his arm around my shoulders. "Come on, mate. It's not that bad."

"Says who? This is a nightmare! I'm trapped in an episode of *Survivor* in the outback! And I don't even get to win the cash at the end!" I was trying to be really mad—but I just wanted to be hugged. And it took every bit of my strength not to just hurl myself into his arms.

"Come on—it's too hot out here. Want some lunch?"

I shook my head. "I just want to be alone for the rest of my life. I never, ever want to have to face another human being. And like that would be hard out here! At least I'm in the right spot!"

He chuckled as we started to walk back. "I've got to go down to Callie's to help her dad with something. I'm taking Jace. You wanna come?"

"Does Callie's mom have radio?" He screwed up his face and I had my answer. "Then I'll wait here, thank you very much."

After they all went their merry way I wandered around the house looking for somewhere cool. And far away from the radio. I should have thought to ask if Callie's place had air con. I finally found a corner of the porch that was in the shade and had this rickety old sun lounge. I tried it and it didn't crash to the ground. Wonders would never cease!

Carefully I flopped onto it and closed my eyes. It wasn't great. It wasn't even good. But it was okay. . . . Then another wave of cramps kicked in. And with them came the realization that another problem was making itself felt.

Oh! Just make it all go away!

Maybe this was some kind of test. . . .

I opened one eye, half expecting to see some weirdo with horns and a giant fork and a bad nineties hairstyle pop up to make me a good deal on my soul in exchange for freedom.

Nah . . . Not even for the complimentary set of steak knives . . .

Or even a lifetime of free Viennese lattes from Starbucks. My mouth started to water for a tall mango-orange iced tea . . . with whipped cream. . . .

My eyes dropped shut again. It was just too hot to hold them open.

Maybe I watched too much television.

Maybe I was delirious.

I just hoped the weird guy with horns didn't have any chocolate.

Chapter Seven

I woke with a start when I kind of felt someone near me. At first I was confused. Then I remembered where I was. *My Big Fat Australian Nightmare*. And I had the lead role. "Oh, it's you."

At first he seemed to be staring really hard at me—specifically at my hair. What was wrong with my hair? Oh—I remembered I'd forgotten to brush it properly after the shower from hell.

Then his eyes dropped to my face and he smiled. Why did the guy always have to smile? Didn't he ever get snarky? Ever? And why did he always smile that slow, lazy smile? Why did it always curl around me like a warm kitten?

Why did I have so many questions?

It was the heat.

"Good to see your little sleep made you feel better," he said dryly.

"There is no law that says you have to wake up happy. Why do people make such a big deal out of it? Would *you* feel better if you woke up and realized that your nightmare was better than your life?"

He chuckled. Such a nice chuckle.

I stretched and sat up. "Hey, it's a bit cooler. And dull."

"It's gonna rain. We'll get a pretty good downpour tonight. It'll cool things right down."

"Don't count on it. I'm here. The clouds'll just hang around and tease us and then run away without offering a measly drop."

He squatted down on the end of the sun lounge. His voice was always soft, always rumbly. "Hey, I got a surprise for you. Two of them."

"You remembered you've got air conditioning and an inside bathroom? No? How about: 'Madeline, you're gonna be airlifted out of here and you have three minutes to pack'? No?"

"Better."

His smile was contagious. "Better than indoor plumbing?"

His smile got wider and he pulled his hand from behind his back. On it sat a swirly-colored foil-wrapped Easter egg. "Chocolate." My face must have been really crazy, because then he burst out laughing. "I know you need chocolate—and I remembered I had this. It's okay. It's been shoved in the back of the freezer."

That was something my brain would never get

around. "You've had chocolate for, like"—I did the math—"*eight months* and you didn't eat it?"

He shrugged. "Must have been keeping it for something special."

Special? "Oh—then I really can't—"

He took my hand and put the egg in mine. It was cold. It would be just the way I love my chocolate: cold and crunchy. "You can, Maddie. I can't think of anything more special."

"Oooooh . . . This is, like . . . well . . . the sweetest thing anyone has ever done for me." This time I didn't fight any natural urges—I *did* hurl myself at him. And I hugged him hard. I couldn't think of a time anyone had been nicer to me, and that stupid lump crept back up into my throat.

Mitch hugged me back and we just sat there listening to some thunder start up somewhere far away. When I'd gotten myself back together I pulled back. "Thank you."

His smile was back. "There's more. . . ."

He dug into his pocket and, okay, maybe I was growing up just a teeny bit because it took a whole thirty seconds before I even considered that he might have been digging for an engagement ring. What he pulled out was even better. "Midol?"

He grinned. "Callie's mum had some."

Wow. Chocolate and Midol. I would survive after all. Of course my tummy would take that moment to gurgle. Ouch. Maybe I should postpone the victory lap. There was one more major hurdle to get over, and if I didn't do something fast it was going to be very embarrassing. And, okay, there are people who'd think I should be used to major embarrassment by now—but this was a biggie. *The* big one. The one from which there was no return. I was going to have to finally visit the bathroom from hell.

Because trust me: passing gas in front of the guy you have the absolute hots for is the one thing you never, ever recover from. The only option left would be to enter a convent. Or maybe work as a missionary in the depths of Africa and have to sew all your own clothes.

It was *that* bad.

I started to climb off the lounge as carefully as I could. There was only one good thing about being a girl and having periods—and that was that guys usually got either freaked by them or they were more sympathetic than any other girl would be. I had a feeling Mitch was type number two.

Testing that theory, I moaned a bit. Just a bit . . . My mother the rabid feminist would have disowned me.

"Are you okay?" Yes, there was panic in his voice. Bingo.

"Yeah—kinda. Um, I don't suppose Callie is still here?" I held my breath as I waited for the answer, because my second and only other choice was the Brat.

He raced off and Callie came running. She stared at my hair too. Well, hello? It's not like she was really in a position to compare.

I got past that and, trying to stay as calm as possible, I

told Callie my dilemma. Of course, I left out the passing-gas-in-front-of-your-loved-one part. Of course, again Callie failed to see there was a problem, but considering that she saw me as some kind of exotic goddess and wanted to do everything possible to make my life easier, she led the way.

Head down, I made sure my Nike-encased feet stepped only wherever her feet stepped. Actually, we saw nothing that moved at all—save for the flies, whose buzzing had become a way of life for me now. So had waving them off. I could just see myself in a few weeks standing on Fifth Avenue waiting at pedestrian lights, shooing nonexistent flies! Like the men in white coats were gonna believe that!

Almost there, Callie turned and handed me the clown nose. "Mitch said to give you this."

Great. Was there anything the guy didn't know? "Sheesh! My life isn't just an open book—it's playing at every cinema near you! In Panavision!"

Callie giggled. "You're so funny, Madeline."

I didn't feel funny, but somehow I was giggling a bit too, and some of the tension between us disappeared.

The nose did nothing to disguise the smell, and if it did, then, man, I didn't want to know about it. There was a wooden floor—thank goodness—and a wooden seat. Under that was just a big hole in the ground. My heart was already racing, and I hadn't even stepped inside! It was dark and I made Callie check everywhere for anything deadly. "Well, like, how would I recognize them? Better for it to be you. Though I suppose those giant Redbacks would be hard to miss . . ."

Callie started to choke. "Giant Redbacks? Maddie—they're tiny! They're like maybe half an inch at their biggest!"

"Really?" That didn't help. At least when I thought they were big I figured I'd see them first. But they were tiny? Eeeooowww. Another shudder ran though me.

As always Callie was very patient with me—though I did give her a "moment" when I grabbed her from behind in a headlock and madly pointing toward the roof, screamed, "Snake!"

When she could finally see—and breathe—she frowned and shook her head. "It's flypaper, Maddie! That strip hanging down is sticky and the flies land on it and stick to it."

"Eowww. Those are dead flies? How disgusting! Don't you ever take it down? Like, could you do it right now? Before I go in? What if they fall on me? Ugh!"

"We take 'em down when they're full. By that time the spiders have usually had a feed."

My stomach rolled. "Oh, puleese . . . Make it all stop!" I turned to go. "I can't do this. . . ."

Of course I could, and I did. And I probably needed that hefty shove from Callie. One day I'd probably thank her—no doubt it would be part of my recovery therapy. As I gingerly sat down, my eyes fell on a rifle hanging on the wall. "Callie? You haven't gone anywhere, have you?"

"I'm here, Maddie."

Maddie? I gritted my teeth. At this rate I'd need crowns by the time we got home. "What's with the rifle?"

"It's just in case."

I waited, shaking my head in the dark interior. "And?"

"Well, just in case you need it. Like if a king brown had a go at ya or something. Sometimes wild pigs. They're pretty nasty."

"But it's not, like, ever, ever needed, right?"

"Oh, yeah! Stan had a King Brown snake have its babies in the back of the loo—"

"Loo?"

"Toilet to you. Anyway, she had her babies behind the seat and she came back and had a go at Stan. They're deadly, ya know."

"Deadly. . . . Eeeaaahhh." My whole body shuddered. My legs shot up and folded themselves Indian-style. I felt faint but I couldn't breathe deeper or I'd die of stinky-air poisoning.

I was done. I was done forever. I would never come back here. I just could not. I wouldn't eat a single thing. That meant I would never need to pass one more single thing.

I beat Callie back to the house; I was a blur. And I scrubbed my hands and arms so hard I could have performed surgery at any major hospital and not been questioned.

I didn't even wig out when the Brat pointed out that my hair now had orange stripes. So that's what Callie and Mitch had been staring at. Yes, again it was the minerals. It didn't affect everyone—just people with fair hair that had dye in it. And of course, how many of us here had blond hair with dye in it? Only one. Me

It was a plot! But I said nothing—which worried them all a bit, I think.

And if I was quiet for the rest of the afternoon, they probably put it down to other things. Only *I* knew I was in shock. Never again would I take anything for granted. And I would devote my entire life to seeing that a monument was erected in Central Park to honor the one true hero of the modern world: the inventor of indoor plumbing.

The smells pulled me back to the present. Callie and the guys were getting dinner ready, and the delicious aromas drifted my way—which was probably a first for this place!

The Brat was helping—he was right there having a ball. I watched him for a while; he really seemed to like being with Mitch. Well, so did I—so I guess I could understand that. But Mitch really seemed to get along with him, too. The Brat was a kid—but Mitch listened to him and laughed at what he said.

Why hadn't I liked the Brat? That actually wasn't true. He was a fair target—and he didn't let me get away with much. I liked people who could take it and give it back. I watched his face light up at something and couldn't help but smile. The Brat would be a lady-killer himself one day. Maybe I could handle having a brother like him. . . . I might even like it. . . .

I guessed I hadn't even given him a chance. I'd just lumped him in with his dad. *Everyone associated with the enemy step to the other side of the room, 'cause we don't like you.* . . .

Pretty lame, now that I thought about it . . .

I refused dinner even though it killed me. Callie kept on at me. She still amazed me—she put up with this every day of her life. And drat it all, she was a really good cook. That food aroma was just torturing me! So I ate. And, man, even though these people did weird things like put jelly and cream on their biscuits, it was the best food I'd had in . . . well, forever.

It was still light when the rain started. It pinged on the old iron roof, and in seconds it was thundering. Almost straightaway the air was, like, twenty degrees cooler!

"Will it crash the roof down?" I had to yell to be heard.

Callie and Mitch laughed. "Nah!" Mitch yelled back. "Come outside!"

"Outside where? To watch the rain? Man, you *have* to get a television!"

He laughed and grabbed my hand and dragged me out to the porch. Then with a huge whoop he ran out into the yard and just let the water pour down all over him. He was jumping and laughing and yahooing like a crazy guy.

I swear, it was impossible to stand there and not laugh with him. Okay, for entertainment it didn't rate against *American Idol*—but it *was* funny. But then again . . . why did I watch *AI*? To check out the up-and-coming musical talent? Or to check out the up-and-coming hot guy talent? Anyone who doesn't know the immediate answer to that question isn't an almost-sixteen-year-old girl with a pulse! So maybe this was just as good. . . .

Better, even. This time there wasn't a glass screen and a thousand miles separating me from the most gorgeous guy I'd ever seen. And it didn't even matter if he couldn't sing!

While I stood there trying to wrap my brain around all this, the Brat raced out there too! "Is this, like, a Y-chromosome thing? A guy thing? Call me slow, but in New York, when it rains we all run to get out of it!"

I was shaking my head at them when a blast of noise from behind sent me whirling around. Callie had brought out a dinky little portable radio, and some really old-fashioned music—it must have been from at least the eighties—blared out in competition with the rain.

I was about to tell her that guys were totally clueless when she raced out there too!

And I was left standing there on the porch, the only dry one. The only one with any sense . . . Alone . . .

They were having so much fun! For a minute I didn't know what to do. Stand there like a geek? Go back inside?

Go and join them?

In the end I didn't have to make the choice.

When I told Reesa what happened next I'd say that I hadn't seen it coming—but of course I had; I just pretended to be surprised when Mitch darted back out of the rain, grabbed me, and dragged me back out there with him.

Of course I screamed—well, who wouldn't? I'd been slowly baking in this sauna they called a climate for three days! The cool water was a shock. Apart from that I think it was the expected girlie thing to do. Guys love it when they think they've caught us unawares. (Guy Psychology 101: *YM* mag, Special Edition.)

The water soaked right through my clothes—what there was of them—sizzling on my burning flesh and slamming my hair down flat on my head. It ran in rivers down over my face and I tipped back to taste it. So sweet! So clean . . .

And then I laughed. Really laughed. Totally cracked up. I couldn't remember when I'd laughed like this—not just a breaker-switch laugh, but a real laugh.

And I couldn't remember ever feeling so alive. . . .

I squealed again when I saw kangaroos jumping around not so far away from us down in those "paddocks." Real live kangaroos! Not fat, lazy zoo ones, but real ones. They'd come out of wherever they hide and were jumping around in the rain too. Mitch said they were looking for food—grasses that would be sweeter in the rain.

I couldn't take my eyes off them. Just magic!

Mitch grabbed me again then, and while it took me a

117

few minutes to work out what he was doing, I finally realized we were dancing to the music. Real old-fashioned dancing, where the guy actually holds you. Of course, I couldn't do it, but who cared? Bumping into him when we made another mistake was even more fun than the real thing!

It was an even bigger hoot when I saw Callie and the Brat dancing too. The Brat cut in on us, and I thought he was going to dance with *me*. But at the last minute he grabbed Mitch and they were doing this really exaggerated guy/girl stuff that was just funnier than anything I'd ever seen.

The Brat was playing the part of the girl, and he kept curtsying and pretending to be coy while Mitch kept bowing and twirling his pretend mustache. They were taking these big, clumsy steps when they danced, and it was a total crack-up. Man, they could really let go. It was hard to believe they barely knew each other. . . .

And I had to give the Brat some points—he had personality. Truckloads. No denying it.

Of course, with Mitch that wasn't even a question. . .

Callie wasn't going to be outdone, so she grabbed me to dance, and I got in on it, and then we all swapped again and it was me and the Brat and Mitch and Callie and then all over again!

Maybe my friends at home wouldn't get it. Maybe it was one of those *you had to be there* kind of things. But me? I couldn't believe it. I laughed till I cried and till I hurt everywhere. It was the best time I could ever remember having—and I had weirdo stripy hair and no makeup and I was drenched to the skin. Go figure.

We stayed outside till way after it got dark and it even started to get cold. Could you believe it? Cold, out there in the world's own natural sauna! And I swear I didn't imagine it when Mitch and I had our last dance and he held me closer. It was just magic—the sweet smell of the rain, the sweet smell of Mitch . . . his smile. I laughed into his eyes, watching the streams of water run over his face and down over his chest.

And I stared at those lips. . . .

And I swear I felt this little feathery kiss right at my temple. Maybe it was his breath on my wet hair. Maybe some blowfly got stuck there for a moment. But I didn't think so.

Inside we raced to get dry and into clean clothes. And, okay, yes, I was jealous when Mitch gave Callie a T-shirt and some of his old shorts to put on. But nothing could take away that warm, gooey feeing that you get when something really special has happened.

Nothing could take away the fact that I couldn't stop the smile every time I thought of Mitch. Or looked at him.

Or those secret little smiles he shot back at me. Nothing would ever take that away.

"Who wants a cuppa?"

Callie's voice pulled me out of my faraway world. Tea. Okay. It suddenly seemed funny to be thinking about stuff as ordinary as a cup of tea. Life was weird sometimes. "Sure, I'm in."

I'd never drunk so much tea in my life. And when I had it was fancy stuff with Mom and Kitty—stuff like vanilla-bean tea and chai and wild blackberry. This was nothing like that—but it would still be my fifth cup that day! These people lived on the stuff. I kept secretly hoping someone was going to pull out some diet Coke—but no such luck. So I lined up for my fifth hit and a chunk of this great cake Callie's mum sent up.

What was kinda cool was that everyone always seemed to sit at the table. Together. When Mitch sat down with his "cuppa" (right next to me) he flicked a pack of cards onto the table. "Anyone want a game? Gin? Poker?"

"Snap?" I offered.

The others voted for poker. Mitch looked over at me. "You okay with that?" he asked softly. "We're only play-ing for buttons—and we'll go easy."

"I'm okay. What makes you think I need going easy on?"

The Brat snorted his "cuppa" and sprayed the table with cake crumbs. "Ever heard of 'poker face,' Made-line? It means people don't know what you're thinking. Like you could ever have a poker face."

"Oh, sooo amusing." Everyone else laughed. I yawned.

"Go easy on her, mate. She can't help being a Park Avenue princess."

"Park Avenue drama queen, you mean!" The Brat was obviously in fine form.

"You might have to eat those words, Brat."

"Ohhh, shakin' . . ."

Callie smacked him. "Don't worry, Maddie. I'll help you if you want."

"Thank you, Calliopie. But I think the Brat has issued a challenge. Or maybe he's just being snarky because he can't play very well. That it, Brat?"

Mitch had been quietly chuckling through all this. Not that I was fooled. He was on the Brat's side—even if I did notice that his arm accidentally-on-purpose bumped into mine too many times for it to be coincidence. Not that I moved away or anything.

He looked at the other two. "Draw poker? Okay with you, Jace?"

Mitch shuffled and dealt the cards while Callie doled out equal shares of buttons and they set the limit. I didn't look at my cards straight off; instead I watched everyone else.

Mitch looked over and offered to help with a few instructions.

I shrugged. "Okay. Doesn't sound too hard."

The Brat snorted again. Callie just smiled and nodded encouragingly.

We all called for our cards and I watched how many everyone else took. I took two. We started putting our bets down. Mitch threw in two buttons. The Brat whooped. "I see your two and raise you three."

Callie called. I raised to six buttons.

"Oooh, we've got a big hitter here, guys!" The Brat chuckled.

Callie folded first. Finally it got too much for the Brat, and he was next to fold.

That left me and Mitch. I upped the ante. He raised his eyebrows. "Okay—showtime."

I put down my three-of-a-kind. It beat his two pairs.

"You bet all that on that hand? Pretty risky!"

"Not if you win it isn't."

I saw him frown then.

"It's only beginner's luck!" That was the Brat, who wasn't looking happy as I dragged all the buttons my way.

Mitch was looking at me with a funny gleam in his eye. After I cleaned up the second time, the gleam had turned to a grin and a knowing nod.

"Jeez! Talk about dumb luck!"

"Thank you, Brat. Don't worry; I'm sure it'll rub off soon. . . ."

After the sixth hand the pile of buttons in front of me was just a tad embarrassing. Just a teeny tad . . .

By now Mitch was laughing out loud, and I just loved that he was looking at me like I was the coolest thing he had ever seen. Was that one of the things he wanted in the woman of his dreams? Someone great at poker? Then, baby, I had it in the bag!

The Brat was really snarky. *He-he-he-he.* "Why didn't you tell us you could play like that?"

"Why didn't you ask?"

The Brat was *not* happy. Good. It would be good for his emotional development to be beaten by a girl. "You wouldn't have told us anyway—even if we had asked! You're a hustler!"

"Oh, bite me. Besides, I would have gone a lot easier on you if you hadn't jumped straight to the conclusion that I'd be hopeless."

Mitch was still laughing. "Great bluff! Maybe we should call you the Park Avenue poker queen! Where'd you learn to play like that? Not at that fancy school you go to?"

"Babysitters. I had a lot when I was a kid. Mom was always at work. B.J. was my favorite—she was like this really sweet granny till Mom walked out the door. Then she'd put on her eyeshade and pull out her cigar and the cards. She used to bet me my pocket money. She was soooo good. She taught me everything I know. The day I beat her for the first time she handed over this bankbook with all the money in it she'd ever won from me."

The Brat's eyes were shining. "That's so cool."

"Yeah. After she got too sick to sit me, I used to still go and play cards with her. Then I'd play all my other babysitters—I'd bet them double-or-nothing what my mom was paying them. It was like taking candy from babies. Mom found out when no one would sit me—and she took my cards away."

Mitch smiled. "Fair dinkum. Yeah . . . I can just see you as a smart little kid. . . ."

I loved it when he said "fair dinkum." I heard Russell Crowe say it once too—it was so cool! I was going say it all the time when I got back home, but I figured it wouldn't be the same.

Mitch was looking impressed—and my insides turned back to warmed honey again. Dreamily I thought about the dance in the rain and that little sneaky kiss. For a day that had started out so badly, it had certainly gotten better.

I grinned back at them. "Who's up for Snap?"

It ended up being a wild choice. "You guys are maniacs! Next time remind me to take out accident-and-injury insurance!"

The Brat and Mitch were determined to win at any cost. It was war. And it was hilarious.

When Callie got up to go I was shocked to realize it was only nine-thirty. Out here time seemed to last longer or something. It was majorly weird, but it was like the clocks moved more slowly. That was both good and bad. . . .

Teeth cleaned, I wandered back to the bedroom and stared at the blue silk Tweety Pie camisole jammies. Would they be too hot? The rain had stopped and someone had cranked the sauna back up to full speed.

Note to self: Silk and suffocating heat do not mix.

P.S. to self: Why don't they teach us this stuff in science?

P.P.S. to self: Then again . . . what's more important: looking good or being comfortable? Heaven forbid there'd be a house fire and the hunky firemen would have to rescue me in, say, Mom's old T-shirt. The headlines would be just too humiliating: *Girl in ugly pajamas rescued from burning building.* Vogue *magazine spokesperson said girl should have been left there.*

I reached for the PJs; the vote was in—I could simply not risk being excommunicated by *Vogue*. The jammies stuck to me everywhere, but I refused to risk my reputation.

Then I groaned, and wished my sense of style were the only thing I was risking. Smacking myself in the head for not getting Callie to walk me out to what I now thought of as "the loo of horrors," I opened the door to the hall and walked straight into Mitch. *Eeowww.* I hoped he hadn't been peeking or anything! I checked the door—it looked pretty solid. Whew. I'd hate for him to have seen me even *thinking* about wearing Mom's old T-shirt.

"Hi." That smile was doing it to me again. . . .

It somehow primed this really romantic music that just seemed to burst into my head. "Hi back."

We kinda stood there just looking at each other for a minute—it would have been great if I didn't have some other concerns. "Um . . . can I do anything . . . ?"

He shook his head. "Um, yeah. I mean, no." He laughed. "I just thought you might need this."

"This" was a bucket. Huh? The romantic music went off-key and screeched to a stop. "You want me to clean? Wash floors? I don't do floors—that's what maid service is for."

He laughed, and I totally loved the way he did that. Even if I couldn't see anything *remotely* amusing in what I'd said. "It's to use to . . . you know . . ."

I didn't know. "Should we try charades?"

125

He sighed. "To pee in . . ."

"Oh." I took the green plastic bucket. (What was it about this country and pukey green?) "You got me my own indoor 'loo'? Callie told me the toilet is a loo! And I have my own? That is so cool . . . I think."

"Mum uses one sometimes. It's okay." He shuffled from foot to foot and shoved his hands in the back of his jeans, which made the muscles in his arms stand out.

I stared at those muscles. Actually I didn't know what else to say or do; needless to say, when I was planning to find out as much as I could about Mitch, this probably wasn't the information I had in mind.

Finally I licked my lips and did one of those goofy grin-type-shrug things. "Okay! Great! Thanks!"

When I closed the door, I leaned against it. Once I scrubbed the images of his mom out of my head, I knew I was going to see this as a romantic moment. The guy was thinking of my deepest problems (well, some of them). And he was trying to help.

It was just that . . . The big rush of air that blew out emptied my lungs completely. *Ohhhhh!* Was it too much to ask that we could have just *one* romantic encounter that didn't involve my most basic bodily functions?

Chapter Eight

The next morning I got up happy that at least all the culture shocks were behind me. Like, what else could happen? I was over all the drama. Now I'd focus totally on Mitch and where our relationship was headed. Because now at least I knew one thing: we were definitely *in* a relationship.

I figured that if a guy gives you a pee bucket, it has to be serious. I thought back to gifts my old boyfriends had given me to prove their love, and this was totally the coolest one. (Not that I'm materialistic or anything . . . I always told them that the gifts were optional. But it did help me judge how much they really loved me.)

Shelley started us all on it. She says you should judge a gift by its resale value. My bucket wouldn't bring me one cent. But it was worth more to me than anything else anyone had given me.

Actually, the bucket had given me a great idea. Well,

not *that* particular bucket—*eeeooww*—but hopefully another one.

It was the earliest I'd been up since we'd arrived, and it was a bit of a freak-out to march into the kitchen and find them all up, showered, and breakfasted—Callie included. It was quarter to eight in the morning! Weren't these people on vacation? Hadn't they heard of sleeping in till noon and then sending out for pizza? Oh. Stop. My brain skidded backward and gave a little blip noise like your computer does when you try to make it do three functions at once. Oh, okay. Keep up, Madeline. No pizza, remember?

Dang.

I focused on Callie. Her being there was a good thing, and after my shower (which didn't include any water going near my hair or face) I got her to work on my next plan. We took warm kitchen water into the yard and we washed my hair there.

It was a pretty jazzed feeling to be taking back some control. It was powerful—like there was nothing I couldn't do! Next job was to find Mitch and drop some very strong hints that he would love to brush my hair out for me. I pictured us lazing somewhere under a tree—preferably one with anticritter netting or fencing around it—talking about how amazing it was that we found each other.

As if he'd picked up my thought signals, he suddenly came around the corner of the house. I smiled my best *how can you resist me?* smile.

He grinned. "Gidday."

Be still, my beating heart. "Gidday back." Like, how Australian was that! I could speak his language! I was feeling totally high then and was just about to tell him how much he wanted to brush my hair when I saw his hands. They were black! Just like last night that romantic music screeched to a halt. "Aaaacck! You can't touch my hair with those hands."

"I wasn't going to—"

"Yes, you were! You were going to . . ." Oh. That's right; he didn't know that bit yet. . . . Drat.

His frown said it all. "Mad, are you okay? Is it the heat? Are you drinking enough water?"

Was water the answer to everything? "No. Yes. No. And the reason for the last is that there are chewy things in your water. And, no—*do not* tell me what they are. I'm already on information overload since I got here, and I figure any more of these little homey details will send me into total brain frizz."

He was still frowning, and I rolled my eyes. We weren't back to him thinking I was a loony again, were we? I thought we'd passed that! Ugh . . . Why were relationships such hard work?

"Um . . ." he began, "I was really just coming to see—"

"Ready, Mitch?" That was the Brat. He was wandering over to us and he was covered in black gunk as well. And he was pretty tickled about something. "Hey, Maddie! Mitch's teaching me to ride one of his motorbikes!"

"What?" Don't ask me why my heart suddenly jumped out of my chest, but it did. Like, what did I care if the kid broke his neck? But my mouth was saying something different. "I don't know. . . . Your dad asked me to look out for you. Bikes can be dangerous." It must have been something in my voice, but both the guys stared at me.

"I'm not gonna get hurt, Maddie."

"I'll look after him—I won't let him do anything stupid."

I still wasn't sure. This time I was looking right at Mitch—searching for that kind of Mitch-thing that always made me feel like everything would be okay. "You promise?"

He nodded. Okay—I felt a bit better, but I still hated this weird feeling that had come over me.

The Brat grinned. "Hey, I'll take all the heat with Dad. I'll tell him it was all my own idea."

I didn't even know I was chewing my lip till I felt a little pinch where my teeth dug in a bit too deep. "It's not that. I just don't want you to get hu . . ."

His grin faded. I couldn't finish, but he still stared at me for ages. "It's okay, Maddie. I'll be okay," he said softly. He turned to go. "But, hey—thanks anyway."

Okay—so what had just happened here? Like, had lightning just struck and I was suddenly the good fairy? Whatever happened to being asked if I wanted the job? Oh, jeez! I wasn't going to have to wear pale pink, was I? Hot pink would be okay—but not any other shade. Oh, perhaps watermelon . . . but no other.

I sighed. I was kidding myself. I knew exactly what had happened. I'd turned into a sister. A big sister. Problem was, I wasn't sure I was ready for it. . . .

How did sisters act? Oh, God. Would I have to take a course? Like summer driving school? Maybe I'd have to rethink all this. . . .

So much for our simple overseas vacation where my only aims were to make my mother see sense over this dumb Barry thing, and soak up as much five-star treatment as I could. Life couldn't be that simple, could it? No, I had to go and fall in love and then turn into some totally lame big sister! I swung back to the house, where Callie waited on the porch. Not to mention sharing my vast knowledge of fashion and makeup. So much to do—so little time!

"Come on, Callie. We've got work to do."

So I was going to be Mitchless. All day. And just when we were both headed in the same direction at the same time: the path to true love. I suddenly knew what those metaphors were that Mr. Johnson kept yammering on about. Because I felt just like a balloon that someone had stuck a pin in—like my head was spinning in crazy circles and then I'd landed with a splat in the corner. Okay, maybe it wasn't quite that bad. Then again . . .

I'd have to distract myself. First I raided my mom's suitcases. I didn't find a lot, but it was better than nothing. And by some miracle of miracles, my waxing kit was still in my suitcase as well.

"What are we doing?"

Kaz Delaney

"Giving you a makeover."

"Oh."

She was wearing shorts and I looked at her legs. Now there was a job screaming to be done. "Ever been waxed? No? We'll start there."

The poor sweetie was probably just too overwhelmed to thank me properly, so I didn't push it—I just shoved her onto the bed instead.

"Will it hurt?"

"Hardly at all." I always think it's better not to dwell on some things. While I waited for the wax to heat, I looked at her hair and eyebrows and nails. There was a fair bit of work to do.

I had no idea why she looked so terrified.

We got the legs done with a minimal amount of screaming. I told her the first time was always the worst. But I knew it had been worth it when she looked pretty jazzed about the end product. She kept rubbing her hands over her calves, saying they'd never been that smooth.

Maybe I got a bit carried away with that positive reaction, because once I'd done her eyebrows and underarms and applied a light coating of mom's spare makeup (which I would never be caught dead in! Blue eye shadow? Hello! Mom, we're in the twenty-first century! Your beautician is robbing you!) I was determined to make this girl a goddess.

"You want to do *what*?" Why did she sound so horrified?

"Your bikini line," I explained calmly.

"But I don't wear a bikini."

"Like that's a reason!" How did I explain to this girl that every woman was responsible for her own beauty—that even if no one ever saw it, it made you feel good about yourself?

I must have worked it out, because she agreed. At least, I think she agreed. And besides, I was only doing her groin. There was no way I was doing a Brazilian! I wouldn't even do that to someone I'd known all my life!

"Relax, Callie. It'll only hurt more if you tense up like that. . . ."

"I'm trying! Do you get this done, Maddie? Who does yours?"

"I go to a spa and they do it there. Mostly I go with my mom's friend Kitty, because Mom's away a lot. Kitty won't ever have kids, and I think she kind of adopted me as hers."

"Your friend can't have children? That's sad. I want a heap of kids."

"Really? Oh, Kitty could if she wanted to. She just chose not to. She's gay. Lesbian. Lie still."

It turned out it wasn't her who had to be still—it was me. A darned stinging beastie chose that moment to sink its talons into me, and I jerked forward with such force the brush shot out of my hand and some hot wax landed in her belly button. Oops. Tricky. Maybe she wouldn't notice.

"Ouch!"

She noticed.

"Sorry."

She nodded at me and I saw her swallow deeply and blink back what looked like a tear. "It's okay. And I understand about your mom's friend. Bruce was gay, too."

"Bruce?"

"Yeah, that's why Mitch came out to get you and your folks the other day, 'cause Stan was helping Dad with what was left of Bruce."

Her sadness wasn't hard to catch. She looked really miserable. "He's dead?"

"Yeah. And Dad didn't take it real well. Dad was real close to Bruce. He raised him himself. It was hard, but Dad says there's no room for poofters out here."

I patted her hand, but it didn't seem enough. "Oh, Cal. I'm so sorry. How did he die?"

"Dad shot him."

"Shot!" My brain slammed on the brakes. I was mid-rip, but even Callie's yelp didn't register. Neither did the teeny bits of her flesh hanging off the wax. All the energy drained from my legs and I fell back onto a chair. "H-he . . . s-shot him? For being gay? Your dad shot Bruce *for being homosexual*?"

Callie was rolling around on the bed, rubbing at the newly waxed area. There wasn't much blood, just a drop or two. "It wasn't like it was the first time—but just that this one was a bit harder 'cause it was Bruce. Oouuch, that hurts!"

"Aaaaack! Focus on the main issue here, Callie! I

don't believe this! Your dad has shot other homosexuals?" The blood was draining from my body and shooting straight to my head, which was thumping.

"Well, they're no good out here, Maddie. What are we supposed to do with them? Everyone has to earn their keep out here."

I clutched at my heart. "They can do anything anybody else can! And often they have a great sense of style! Haven't you ever seen *Queer Eye for the Straight Guy*? Like, th-that ugly shower thing could be a tropical paradise complete with mirror tiles, loofah rack, and a built-in outdoor juice bar! You have to talk to your dad!"

She stopped rolling. "Bruce couldn't do that. . . ."

"How do you know?" My eyes widened.

Callie pushed up on her elbows. She had to stop frowning like that—she'd have furrows you could plant crops in by the time she was thirty. Maybe she was just realizing that her dad wasn't playing with all his marbles. The only thing wrong with that theory was that she was looking at me like I was the crazy one! Hellooo?

"Maddie?" she said in that soft slow drawl of hers. "The reason Bruce couldn't do anything out here is that—"

"No one gave him a chance?" I was hysterical. I was way past the Springer show. This was pure Dr. Phil. . . .

"No. It's because Bruce is a bull. He was one of dad's bulls. . . ."

"A . . . bull? A bull? Like an animal? A male cow?" My headache was starting again. "You know, I'm start-

135

ing to really like you people, but sometimes it's like you're from another country!"

"We are."

"Well, like from another universe!"

She was looking really worried. "Maddie? You didn't really think my dad would—"

"Well . . . maybe not," I lied.

She smiled. "Good. Because he never would. Although there was that one time we don't ever mention—when that Bible-bashing bloke came around."

I stopped breathing.

And she burst out laughing. "Gotcha!"

Okay. Very droll. This one was just a misunderstanding. Breathe deep. In and out. I felt my heart rate slow back to normal. Phew. Still shaky, but I was okay, and the best part was that it hadn't involved anything that would bite me.

And if the manicure and paint work on her fingernails and toenails wasn't as perfect as it could have been, I didn't think that was entirely my fault.

It was just a tragedy I didn't get to do more to her hair. But while the feathered bangs around her face gave her a really soft look, I admit, that was a very close call with the scissors and her left eye. Maybe I should've waited till I'd stopped shaking. . . .

My eyes weren't shaking, though, and they were telling me that the improvements were really worth it. With her eyebrows fined down and that soft fringe of hair, she was looking pretty good.

The best thing was that Callie agreed. She just kept staring at the mirror with a dumb grin on her face.

I couldn't stop my own smile. It felt good. Really good. And I'd teach her how to do it all herself—I'd even leave my stuff here. "What can I say? I am an artiste. A thirsty one. You wanna cuppa?"

Callie laughed. "A *cuppa*? Listen to you! Yeah, I'll have a cuppa. And my mum sent up some fruitcake."

"More cake? Don't you, like, count calories or anything?"

"Don't have to. You work it off around here. I've been up since five this morning, doing all my chores. And I had to give my horse a workout too. It gets too hot later in the day at this time of year."

I heard some of her words, but I had to be honest; everything after the words *five A.M.* had been just a blurry buzzing noise. "Aaaack! That's like the middle of the night!"

"You're so funny, Maddie!"

Why did everyone laugh around here? Was it all this tea they drank? Call me a coward, but I couldn't handle any more of these child-torture stories. I needed something I could get my brain around. "Have you got a boyfriend?"

Her face started to glow.

"You have?" I squealed. "You have! Tell me everything."

"Well, he's not really my boyfriend—just a boy that I like."

I cut myself a chunk of cake and figured I'd wake at five in the morning and mentally do Callie's chores with her. Yeah, right. "Is it a guy you go to school with? Does he like you? I want every detail! Come on, girl! Spill!"

Her face was bright red now. "There's nothing to tell."

I waited. But after I minute I realized she meant it. Oh. When Reesa says there's nothing to tell, she means she's waiting for me to pry it out of her. Callie wasn't; Callie just clammed up.

"What about you? You got a boyfriend back home?" she asked.

"Back home? Nah. There was Josh Weiner. He was my last; he was such a loser. But—"

"What's it li— Oh, sorry, Maddie. I interrupted—go on."

"No, it's cool; what were you asking?"

Her eyes were really bright. "Well, I just wanted to know what it's like to live in a city like New York."

Whoa! Here was a topic I could talk about! And I did. And all she did was ask more questions. When I figured she knew as much about New York as I did, I stopped. "Do you want to travel, Callie?"

Her eyes were still bright, but kind of dreamy too. "Yeah. I want to see the world. All of it. Maybe I could come and see you in New York! But then I want to come back here and settle down."

"Why?! Oh, sorry to splutter." I wiped her down. "There—I got all those crumbs."

" 'Cause I love it, Maddie. There's nowhere on earth like this place."

"Yeah, well, you got that bit right." And let's all pray it stayed that way! What we didn't want was for this place to start cloning itself. "You and Mitch are both crazy! I could never leave the city. How can you live without Starbucks and take-out food?"

She laughed. "Easy! I'll show you!" She dived off the chair. "Want to make some damper?"

"*Damper?* That's not like a diaper, is it?"

"Nah! It's bush bread, silly."

My eyes popped. "You want me to bake bread? You want to *bake*?" I clutched at my chest. "I'll be baking bread and wearing no makeup! Aaaack! Is it possible to turn Amish!? Aaaacccck! I'm turning Amish!"

"Come on—it's fun!"

Panic was setting in. I pulled back against the grip she had on my wrist. "No, no, no, Callie. You have it all wrong. Baking is never fun. Baking is, well, *baking*. I think it's *work*. If God had meant us to bake She wouldn't have invented restaurants and coffee shops!"

But Callie wasn't listening, and before I could even scream that I was allergic to all things domestic, I was bashing this flour-ball thing.

Callie laughed. "Not so hard. You have to knead it gently. Like this: push the dough away from you and then roll it back and do it again. Push, roll, and do it again. . . ."

Push, roll, and do it again. . . . Okay, so that bit was cool. "Hey, this is fun!"

She nodded as she oiled a flat tray and added a little

139

more water to my dough. "How come you and your boyfriend broke up?"

"Josh?" I frowned and pushed the dough away again. "He's a rat. I was just imagining that this was his head, actually. You know, this is great therapy!" She was still staring at me with a curious look, and I figured she didn't get much girl-guy talk. "Okay, well, he did heaps of bad stuff. Always pressuring me for, you know, sex. Always trying to make me feel bad for saying no. But then he went too far. He told my entire English class that I had a zit on my butt. I had never been so humiliated. Well, not till I arrived here and discovered myself slap-bang in Humiliation Central. Of course everyone thought he'd actually seen it—which, of course, meant they thought he'd actually seen my butt naked, which, of course, meant they all thought that Josh and I . . . well . . . And we hadn't! Never! I've never—"

"So how did he find out?"

It had been a black day that day. A day I'd never forget. I even tied a black ribbon around the goldfish bowl. "My kinda friend Shelley told him. She's just a girl who hangs out in my group, actually. I don't like her that much—she can be mean. But she said it was an accident. I yelped when I sat down and she said she forgot he was there when she asked if my butt zit was still hurting. . . ."

I'd finished kneading and Callie put Josh's head in the oven—she told me the great thing about bush bread is that you don't have to wait for it to rise. You can cook it right away. Okay, I was cool with that. Very cool. I was starving. Again. What was it with this place? "She must have been real sorry. Your friend."

"Yeah, well, she said she was but I don't know. . . . I was pretty hurt by Josh at the time—totally wigged out. But he really is pond scum and I think she just helped me see that. So I guess it doesn't really matter if she did it on purpose or not."

Callie looked up and started to smile—then she looked harder and burst out laughing.

"What?"

"Look in the mirror!"

"Ohmigod—I'm covered in flour! How did that happen? Well, what did you expect from a bake virgin? It wasn't like I knew what to do!" I narrowed my eyes. "But you, however, are totally clean. . . ."

I saw her look of horror as she started to run. "You wouldn't! No!"

But I did. And it was a perfect shot! She looked like a yeti with two dark eyes peeking out. Then she did what I never thought Callie would do—she picked up a handful of flour and hurled it back!

Now we were both totally covered. What a hoot. My first flour fight . . . We didn't carry it on—although I'd have loved Mitch to walk in that minute. A flour fight with the guy you love would never be a bad thing, I quickly decided.

Laughing, we cleaned up the mess—eeooww, more domestic stuff—and waited for the bread to bake. It was torture! It smelled so good! And when we took it out of the oven and Callie presented this big, puffy round loaf to me, I was totally awestruck. "Mine? I really made this?"

Callie went to break a piece off and I smacked her away. "No, don't touch it—it's perfect! I made this? Wow."

"We *have* to touch it—we have to eat it, silly!"

"No! Never. I'm going to have this bronzed. My first loaf. My first ever baking thing . . . Ohmigod—I know my calling! This was fate. Kismet. Callie? Drumroll: I'm going to be a chef . . . ! Okay, what else can we bake? Let's get at it! What about a bombe Alaska? Or maybe rich Sacher torte with a fresh blueberry coulis and Chantilly cream. That's my favorite dessert. I get it at Selkie's in NY every time we go there. . . . He's really famous for it. Can we make it now?"

Wouldn't you know it? Mitch's mother was all out of fresh blueberries, and I couldn't find one thing in the pantry that said Sacher anything! So we had fresh made-by-Madeline damper bread and jelly that they called jam. They're so precious down here. . . . It was okay. Better than okay, really.

After all that work I was totally zonked—so we found that cool spot on the porch and shared the sun lounge. It was too hot to do anything else, so we just read through my magazines. (I never travel anywhere without them. You just never know when you're going to need advice on how not to be a fashion disaster—or worse—need to take a quiz to know if some hot, droolicious guy loves you.)

We were quiet for a long time, just reading. And thinking. This place gave a person a lot of time to think. . . . Bit spooky, really. "I had heaps of fun today, Callie."

She took a long time to answer. That seemed natural out here—like people had time to really think about their answers. "Me too. I'll miss you when you have to go home. . . ."

I looked down at her—at those big brown eyes that were just a bit lonely. "Yeah. That's what I think too. . . ." I cleared my throat. "Hey—I've got to start this new project when I get back to school. Some of our totally lame teachers think we've forgotten the basics— they think we've forgotten how to use snail mail—that all we can do is text and e-mail. So if I write you real, old-fashioned letters, will you write back?"

She grinned. "You mean it? Sure! And next year we're supposed to get more computers at school and we'll be able to e-mail! Something to do with satellites or something . . ."

"Oh! That is sooo cool! So we can write letters now, and then next year we can e-mail too."

I didn't think I'd ever met anyone like Callie before. Someone who can kind of, like, admire other people but still be really happy in her own skin. She'd be an amazing best friend. . . .

Friends . . . It made me wonder what Mitch and the

Brat were doing. I missed Mitch. I missed that smile and that slow drawl and that wink.

And soon I'd have to leave it all. . . .

"Oh, look, Cal! The sun's going down. It's so beautiful. . . ."

Chapter Nine

Hours later I tossed my electronic diary on the bed. When my dad was reading this one day—and somehow in my heart I never gave up on the thought he would—he'd see that today was the total weirdest day of my entire life.

For starters, I'd baked! Me, baked! Baking had definitely been one of those experiences on my "make-sure-to-miss" list. But, hey, it'd been cool!

Then, okay, there *had* been this über-über-über ghastly moment at dinner when I realized I was eating Bruce. Aaack! Poor gay Bruce. The ultimate humiliation—eaten by straight people . . .

I'm not into meat much anyway. But *occasionally* meat was okay. Well, that stopped tonight. From the moment I set down my fork and refused to have any more Bruce, eating as I knew it ceased to exist. *Occasionally* would never be okay again.

Call me lame, but I never thought much about where meat came from. Sure I knew that sheep and cattle and pigs provided the basics—but it was always a hazy notion. I never associated the actual animals with what was on my plate. Till tonight. Tonight changed everything.

Hello? How did anyone eat something they used to be on first-name terms with? Should I eat our doorman's dog?

That was not cool.

Then there was this weird thing with this place. I hated it. Not hard! There were so many things to hate. I had a list!

And yet a part of me was starting to feel strung up about leaving. . . .

That was waaaay in the weird zone.

And then there was Mitch.

Well, then there was *always* Mitch. . . . I just didn't get the guy. I felt like I was this daisy and there he was plucking off my petals one by one: *I love her; I love her not.*

Last night we slow-danced in the rain and he gave me a pee bucket and today we were barely speaking? Today he avoided me completely? Like I was sooo forgettable?

Was I?

It was raining again, and I fell back on Mitch's pillows and listened. I'd never heard rain stop and start so suddenly; there were just a few drops now. It was so quiet. Callie had gone home; she'd taken some mags with her. I'd give her the lot when I left. . . . The Brat was so pleased with himself—claimed he could ride a bike now.

That's all he and Mitch talked about after their showers. And through dinner. And after dinner. The only other topic had been Bruce—and we could have given that a miss!

I wandered out to get a glass of water and tried not to think about the chewy bits. Maybe I could market it as a complete food: "food and drink in one time-saving gulp." Maybe the space program would be interested.

From the kitchen I could hear voices. Mitch and the Brat were still chatting. . . . I moved closer—I didn't really care what they talking about; I just wanted to hear their voices.

"Maddie? You okay?"

I sighed—I should have known Mitch would hear me; He never missed a thing. "Yeah. I'm okay. . . ."

"Wanna come out here? It's cooler."

Okay, so he was only being a good host. I didn't care—I wandered through the door and flopped on the end of the Brat's camp bed. It was pretty dark out there. "What're you guys doing?" I whispered—which was dumb; there were only the three of us, and we were all wide-awake. But somehow it seemed right to whisper.

"We were talking about our folks, actually." Mitch's voice was low too. He propped himself up on one arm and I could just see his smooth, tanned skin. "Jace was wondering where his dad is. We'll call them in the morning—see if we can pick them up on the truck radio."

My heart did that dumb thing again. "Are you worried, Jace?"

147

Kaz Delaney

"No." He'd said it too fast. I hadn't thought to ask him before—I guess because he'd seemed too jazzed about the whole bike thing. But it was night now, and this place gives you time to think. Here in the dark Jace was thinking. . . .

"They'll be okay, you know. . . ."

"She's right, mate. My old man knows these roads like the back of his hand."

He nodded at us. He didn't speak, but I could see the outline of his head—and I could see that his eyes were maybe a bit too bright.

A lot of stuff was going on in my head as well. "Hey, I guess it's a bit too late, but I never did ask how you felt when you found out about Mom and me. Did it spin you out?"

I heard him take this big sigh. "Yeah—a bit. Dee's really close to Grandma—and I am too—but it's not the same. Since Mum d—since she went, it's kind of been me and my dad. He's my best friend, I guess. We do a lot of stuff together. Dee too—but she's always wanting to do girl stuff with Grandma and our auntie Pam."

I nodded, although I would never see why anyone would want to do *anything* with Auntie Pam. I'd met her once the day after Christmas, but right now wasn't the time to say it. Right now, Jace was hurting. I rubbed his ankle through the sheet, my voice really low. "You're scared my mom will just come in and take him away, aren't you?"

He choked a bit on that, and I felt like the biggest jerk

on earth. Why hadn't I even stopped to think about what this was doing to him?

He didn't say anything for a minute. "Aren't you? Aren't you scared my dad will take all your mom's time?"

I swallowed. My head was still fighting with images of Jason as a little kid of seven losing his mom. Jeez! That would be the total worst. . . . I could feel my eyes burning, and I squeezed them shut but it didn't stop. "Me? Yeah, well—ahem—I, er, didn't really think my mom had any time to have taken. Her life is pretty full." I shrugged. "Okay, so yeah. I did worry. I do worry. Sometimes I think I hardly see her as it is. Sometimes I wish . . ." I shrugged. "Yeah . . . all that . . ."

"What about your dad?" Mitch asked.

His voice had been so soft—like he really cared. I looked across at him. Mitch must have been thinking we were the biggest dorks in history, but he'd asked the question. And he sounded like he really wanted to know, because it was important. "Well, I guess this is the question we'd all like answered. My mom and dad had only one date, and it wasn't the kind where you hear violins and drink champagne." This dumb, unfunny laugh kind of spilled out. "One day I really will be on *Jerry Springer*. . . . The topic will be: 'I was conceived in a petri dish.' Yep—I'm a test-tube tot. A scientific freak."

Mitch whistled low and long. It kind of summed it all up. "Fair dinkum? Do you know anything about him?"

The lump moving from my chest to my throat was probably bigger than this Uluru place they all talked about. I tried to push it back, but it was being totally stubborn. I ignored it—focused on being cool. "Oh, I figured she ticked the boxes that said: tall, dark, handsome, above-average IQ, and no psychotic tendencies or nasty habits that might be passed down—like, say, picking at your teeth or chopping people up and putting them into bowling bags. They'd be the ones I'd pick."

Pretty good. Just a tiny voice crack at the end.

The Brat rolled over and looked right at me. "Are you okay?"

I nodded.

"Are you going to find out?"

The lump tightened, squeezed. . . . "Find out who my father is? Sure, one day. But it's no big deal. I mean, if he cared he would have asked already. I mean, he *did* donate that wriggler over sixteen years ago. . . . It's not like he hasn't had time. I used to dream that I'd be walking down the street one day and this guy would stop and say, 'Hey! You're the image of my mother or my grandmother'—(of course I wouldn't look that old!)—and I'd have found him." I stopped and drew in a shaky breath. "Hey! Let's cheer up here, people! It's not a biggie right? And anyway, wouldn't you know? I already have a pretty good idea. Like I'm pretty sure I know who . . ."

"Who?"

"It's okay, Maddie. . . ." Mitch was moving closer.

One tear escaped. I fought it back—I dragged up my knees and hugged tight. "Well, he's the right age, the right connections, the same chin dimple, and the totally perfect amount of cool. And I have to say he has great hair. And he even looks good in makeup—if you like blue. I *have* to be his daughter. I mean, who could deny it? Can't you guess?" They were staring at me like I'd lost it. "Oh, come on! I am obviously the child of Mel Gibson. . . . It's so clear I don't know why he hasn't heard about it already and come looking for me."

This was where they were supposed to laugh.

No one was laughing.

Not even me.

But I wouldn't cry either. Flannagan women don't cry—we cope.

Mitch squeezed onto the bed and put his arm around me and pulled me in. I reached for Jace, too. He leaned close and there we all sat, huddled together for a long time . . . in the dark, with only the crickets and frogs for company. (I shuddered. At least, I hoped that was all. . . .)

Eventually I wiped my face in Jace's hair. "I'm sorry, *mate*. I haven't made it any easier on you, have I?"

He laughed a funny, teary laugh. "Nah! You were great! You did all the work! I just kept thinking that Dad would decide he couldn't live with a drama queen like you and it'd be all over!"

"You brat!"

He shrugged. "Well, face facts. If we end up doing a Brady Bunch, one of us has to give up a country."

I jumped so hard I smacked their heads together. "Eeek. I always assumed if the worst happened you'd come live with us! I will never give up the United States! Never give up New York City! I was born for it. I love it—it loves me! It's a perfect union! The economy will collapse!"

Mitch was chuckling in my ear, and even as miserable as I was, it felt really good. . . .

"Yeah, well, that's me and Australia. Well, sort of."

"No, you don't understand. For me it's much worse! Me? Live in Australia, forever? I don't speak the language!" I stopped. "Well, okay, on the plus side, the shopping *is* good if you use U.S. dollars—but what good would that do when I haven't seen evidence of a single major department store? Like, where is your Saks? Macy's? I truly cannot exist without them!" I had two guys groaning— one in each ear! "Oh, come on! I'm laying out a potential crisis here. A little bit of sympathy wouldn't hurt!"

That made them laugh more, and I gave up. And I wouldn't have admitted it to them, but they both had great laughs, and it was pretty cool to be sitting here with them. My heroes. Some weird flash of wisdom must have spun off course and hit me instead of whoever it was meant to go to, and in that moment I realized I'd really miss them both. . . .

I sobered. "Jace? I know this is going to sound really dumb, but you know . . . if I could, like, pick a brother . . . it would be you. You're totally über cool." There was that voice crack again. "And 'über cool'? That's my highest compliment, pal. And I'm looking forward to meeting Dee, too."

He grinned back at me. "Yeah—I know what you mean."

Okay, I hadn't had much experience with Hallmark moments, and I was learning they were exhausting. So, much as I hated to do it, I pulled out of Mitch's hug. Later I'd lie in bed and torture myself over that decision—but the truth was, I was tired. Talk about my father did that to me every time. So did studying the face of every guy I passed in New York. Every day.

At least out here there was no one to question. Here I was safe and free. "Okay, guys. I'm off to bed."

Mitch got up as well. "Yep—big day tomorrow. We've got a surprise planned."

I held my hands up and backed away from him. "No, not that. Puleese don't use that kind of language. Puleese don't give me nightmares this close to going to sleep! Ever since I arrived in this country, every time someone says 'surprise,' I suffer."

His perfect white smile reached me in the dark. "No, this is a good one—you'll love it. Promise."

I loved the way he said *promise*. Okay, so I was tired and a bit emotional, but I swear I could hear him saying, "I promise to take you . . ." Now there was a thought to go to sleep on. . . .

I ruffled Jace's hair. "Night, mate."

Mitch's hand was on my back. "I'll come and make sure you don't trip over anything."

"I'll be okay."

He grinned. "I want to."

I couldn't argue with that—even if we only had to walk the length of a very small house.

He kind of kept his arm around me—which was just über über über! What more could I say? At his room we stopped. "Are you going to be okay?"

"Yeah, I'm fine. But thanks."

We were facing each other now, and his arms slid around my waist. Breathing was getting almost impossible, and I'm sure he could hear my heart beat. It was performing the closing bars of some wild Ricky Martin number.

His voice was deep and rumbly—almost a whisper. "If you need anything—or get upset—just come get me. Okay?"

I wanted to nod, but his eyes held mine. Then his head was moving closer . . . slowly . . . his eyes never leaving mine. . . .

I couldn't move.

Then it happened.

His lips met mine.

And I swear my heart exploded. His lips were so soft and so gentle. So sweet. So hot . . .

And then, too soon, he'd pulled away. His forehead rested against mine, his voice that rumbly whisper. "G'night . . ."

He started to move but I pulled at his arm. "M-Mitch? I don't understand. . . . I thought you didn't like me again."

He sighed a deep, tired sigh. "I like you, Maddie. I really like you."

"But why didn't you spend any time with m——?"

He leaned over and kissed me again—just a tiny butterfly kiss. "Because you're fifteen."

"Nearly sixteen!"

"Still fifteen . . . G'night. See you tomorrow."

I don't know how I got from the doorway to the bed. Maybe I floated. Then I just let my body fall backward, and there I lay—unable to move. I wanted to stay awake forever. No! I wanted to sleep so that morning would come faster.

Had anything more romantic *ever* happened to me? Before this my high bar to beat had been when Brad Lawrence pushed me into the gym storage room and kissed me. And I hadn't even known he liked me! Shelley said he was on a dare—but like I believed that. She was just jealous. . . .

And tonight was way beyond that. Brad wasn't even in the zone anymore.

I snatched at my magazines, frantically tossing issues aside till I found the one I wanted. The right page opened straight away because I used it so often. It was my bible, my guide: "Is He in Love?" The title called to me. Three little questions—one miniquiz—and I'd know.

1. The first time he kissed you, did he . . .
   a. Go straight for the grope.

155

b. Feel like a science project—all clinical and tight lips.

c. Kiss you gently right on the mouth.

My response: Check mark for "c". No question—I could still feel it.

2. You've got a killer case of flu (*insert: or have period and someone has stolen your makeup and your hair has turned orange*) and you look like hell. Does he . . .

a. Not even notice.

b. Ask if you always look like that when you're not made-up and keep making noises that sound like he's choking on a chicken bone.

c. Tell you that without makeup and with a swollen nose you look beautiful to him.

My response: Check mark for "c" again! He said he liked me better without makeup!

3. It's time for him to meet the parents. Does he . . .

a. Break out in an itchy rash every time you mention it.

b. Ask if your parents have access to police files and personal records before committing.

c. Act über cool and make a great impression.

My response: Check mark for "c" again! Double ditto! He has met her and she loves him!

I raced to the score page. Three "c"s? Aaaack! He loves me! I had never, ever been so pleased to see a straight-c average! I devoured the words:

He's besotted, babe! He's got it soo bad for you. He is one hot honey—hot for you. But don't make him do all the work! If you want to hang on to him you have to meet him halfway.

Meet him halfway? Did that, like, mean, meet him halfway around the world? Because I'd already done that. Or did it mean . . . My heart lifted its rate and my hands started to feel all clammy. Oh, no . . . I couldn't be . . . If I looked down and saw spots I'd die. It would mean one thing: I was allergic to sex; allergic to even the thought of sex. Maybe I was sexually challenged? Was that the PC term for frigid?

I wished Mom were here. . . .

But she wasn't, and I was going to have to sort it out myself. Mitch's face swam back in front of my eyes. Okay—so it wasn't like I was getting pressure from the guy. (Josh Weiner could take lessons!) Just the opposite, really. It was the ultimate love sacrifice. He was staying away—staying away because I was too irresistible.

I flopped back on the pillows again. Wasn't that every woman's dream? To be too irresistible? That was the ultimate cool.

In a flash it was all so clear. We were a modern Romeo and Juliet: *Mitch and Madeline: An Outback Tale of Love and Suffering.* (Maybe they'd make a movie!)

Our path would be hard. We would suffer for our love—but we would suffer together. . . .

To a point.

As my eyes closed, my mind was busy with this big eraser wiping out the part of the story where one dies. I mean, if I was going to suffer for a guy, then the least he could do was hang around and make it up to me! So easy to see Shakespeare was a man! No woman would let the guy get off that easily!

Chapter Ten

The next morning I was awake just as the sun was rising. I got up and went and sat on the porch outside Mitch's room. It was so peaceful. The air was a bit crisp, but you could feel the heat already starting to kick in. The kangaroos were out again. I knew now that as soon as the sun rose properly they'd disappear till sundown again. I'd never get over the fact that during the day, they were just hanging out in the trees—but somehow you couldn't see them.

I went and made myself a cuppa and came back to sit for a while.

Later on, no one believed it when I was ready first. I'd been told to bring my bikini and a towel, so I figured we were going to swim or something.

In the yard Callie motioned me to get on the back of her bike, but Mitch shook his head. "Cal? I'd better take

Maddie. She hasn't been on a bike before. You take Jace—he's pretty good now. He knows what he's doing."

It was one time I didn't argue about being told I was incompetent. Not when it meant I got to hug Mitch for close to two hours, 'cause that was how long he said it would take to get there. I was pretty sure that was the same reason he'd chosen me, too.

I also didn't argue when he gave me his cowboy hat or when he placed it gently on my head. I knew now it was called an Akubra, and he didn't give me one of the spares—he gave me his, the one he wore everywhere, everyday—and he took the spare. Was that romantic or what?

Of course if Mom knew she'd have a fit that it wasn't a hard hat—which again proved she knew absolutely nothing about love. They did stuff differently out here and I quickly weighed it up: (a) protect myself from head injury or (b) the chance to wear the hat that sat on his head every day; the one that smelled like him; the one filled with all his Mitch-i-ness. There was no contest.

All this topped off a funny morning. Seeing him at breakfast probably should have been weird. I mean, Jace was right there with us, so I couldn't, like, throw myself at him or anything. But he just smiled that lazy smile and sent me one of those bone-melting winks, and I knew it hadn't all been a dream. . . .

"Gidday."

"Gidday back."

Really—after that, who'd have been surprised that I

couldn't wait to get on that bike and get my hands on the guy!

The trip was a bit rough, but that was okay, 'cause I really did have to hang on tight. The roads were just more red or orangey dirt. I was pretty tense at first, but as soon as I realized Mitch knew what he was doing, I just relaxed and went with it. I could tell we were climbing higher, could see the changes in the land and trees and things. More trees for starters, and more of those giant palm things we'd seen on the trip down.

A couple of the trees were amazing. They had no leaves but were covered in these huge white flowers— and I mean covered! Thousands of big, fluffy flowers. But as we got closer I couldn't believe my eyes. All the flowers took off and flew away! They were birds! Big white birds with some yellow on them.

"Cockatoos," Mitch called back.

I watched them till Mitch slowed and pointed over to some other denser trees. "Water buffalo," he yelled.

"Eeeooww. They're huge! And they look like they all missed tickets to the Eminem concert! Not happy! Don't stop!" I clung tighter as we moved off, wondering if those ugly beasties understood English. Like, if one attacked, surely it would make a difference if I told it I was vegetarian. I mean, if I didn't eat them, why should they eat me? Fair was fair. . . . Maybe I should also throw in that I don't wear boots made of crocodile skin? Couldn't hurt . . .

The road sort of ended not long after that, and the

ground was sandy. Through the trees I could see water—like a river, I supposed, but it was pretty wide. Mitch pulled into a clearing and pointed again. I couldn't see what he was looking at—and then one moved. Omigod! All those logs! They were crocodiles! Real live ones! Big, ugly, horrible, should-be-banned crocodiles.

Callie and Jace pulled in alongside us. Jace got off but there was no way my tootsies were setting foot on this ground. I was totally freaked. Mitch wasn't going anywhere either, unless he piggybacked me, because I was not letting him go. Ever! I didn't care if we *were* half a football field away from them—I was not taking chances.

Mitch looked back at me and grinned. "Do you want me to move farther away?"

Everything was shaking—even my voice. "Yes, *much* farther away. I'll tell you when to stop. You might recognize it anyway—the Statue of Liberty will be waving at us!"

"They're slow on land, Maddie."

"Oh, right! And like I want to challenge them to a footrace to prove it! Back! I want back! Farther!"

Jace laughed. "Mad, it's the death roll you have to watch out for. That's how it kills you. It drags you down into the water and rolls over and over with you till you drown—and it takes you to its pantry and stuffs you in and then just snacks on you till you're gone."

"Death roll? That's what Reesa and I always call the hip-roll exercise. Instead it's a . . . ?" I just stopped the jag in time. "Stop! No more! Does everything in my life have to be snatched from me? Even my right to flab-free hips?"

Why could guys never see the seriousness of anything?

"Stop it, you pair! Look at her—she's green! It's okay, Maddie—we'll get moving and get you out of here."

I was so grateful that I made a serious note to make sure Callie is put into my will. Callie could share everything with Reesa—and the red sweater probably wouldn't itch her. We had the same size feet as well—all in all, it would work out perfectly.

It helped that I had this to work out, because I'd refused to open my eyes for the rest of the trip. Thank goodness it was only another half hour, but even so, I refused to open my eyes ever again unless they promised me there were no crocodiles waiting to rock 'n' roll with me.

Mitch turned and whispered low in my ear, "Trust me, okay? I wouldn't let anything happen to you. Now I want you to do me a favor—keep your eyes closed for a ick."

I relaxed again then. Okay—he was probably going to kiss me. And man, I'd been hanging out for it. That's why it was a bit of a shock when he picked me up and I felt us moving.

I went to speak but he cut me off. "Keep them closed, Maddie. I've been dying to show you this . . ."

He let me slide down and then stood behind me, his arms around my shoulders. "Open."

"Oh!" The place totally took my breath away. It was magic. It was crazy. Like, here we were in the middle of this really wild countryside, and this place looked like it had popped up out of some tropical paradise somewhere. Golden sand led down to the most beautiful blue-green water I had ever seen. It was so clear you could see right to the bottom. It was too wide for me to swim across, and it curved and was protected by this huge rock wall that ran about two-thirds of the way around it. Only our side was beachy and accessible. And then there were all these palms and ferns that dipped down to the water.

"It's beautiful. . . ."

I felt him grin into my hair. "I knew you'd like it."

"And it's so quiet." I'd been here all of a minute, and yet I felt the peace wash over me and slow everything down. Even Callie's and Jace's dash into the water didn't spoil anything. The sun beat down, beautiful cool water called to me, and Mitch had his arms around me. It was the only time in my life I'd felt as if a part of my heart might just belong somewhere else but New York City. Only a teeny tiny part . . . Call me a lovesick romantic, but I just knew that teeny, tiny part of my heart wouldn't be coming home with me.

His voice was right at my ear. "We call it the Never Never up here. Not just this place—this whole land that surrounds it."

"The Never Never?"

"Yeah." His breath tickled and tingled against my ear.

"They say once you've experienced the magic of this place, you never, never want to leave."

Wow. I'd just been thinking that. This was spooky, probably the most spiritual moment of my life. Oh, noooo!

The day was a magical blur. We swam, we chased fish, we chased each other, we rode on each other's backs in the water, and we laughed—laughed more than I'd ever laughed in my life . . .

The water was warm on the surface, yet really sharp and chilly deep down. I was floating on my back holding Mitch's hand when I felt his other arm slip around my waist and pull me down. After all these days of being afraid of everything that moved, I didn't even flinch when his hands moved over my skin. I just knew it was him. And I knew I was safe. . . .

This was the totally coolest thing that had ever happened to me. And then it turned into the hottest when he pulled me close and kissed me underwater. Right underwater! I forgot to breathe and he gave me some of his breath. . . .

It was totally the most romantic thing ever. I would never forget it . . . ever.

We floated to the surface with our lips still locked and then he started again. And it was even better. It was long and deep and everything I'd ever dreamed a kiss could be. My whole body shivered even though that blazing sun was beating down on us. . . .

Like in a dream he led me out of the water and we sat

close and ate sandwiches, and I didn't even care if the bread was a bit dry. We built a campfire and made a cuppa in a "billy"—which was like this tin can with a handle that we put on the coals—and for a while I lay out on a rock and just let the peace work its magic.

And I thought about this place—this amazing place. And I thought about Mitch's kisses. They were worth nearly drowning for. . . . Nothing in my whole life had ever topped that moment, and I doubted anything would.

Not even all the little smooches that followed while we lay on the rock or when we went back in the water. These country boys might not grab an opportunity as fast as their city cousins, but when they do they go all out. . . .

No, nothing topped this day.

Luckily I'd finally remembered my digital camera and I got some fab shots. (Well, I hadn't really forgotten it before—but till now, apart from Mitch, I hadn't wanted to photograph anything!) Some old shots were stored there, and I showed them some of Pattie and Jake and some of me and Reesa and a couple of other friends.

And I got great ones of Mitch and me by doing the old hold-the-camera-out-and-shoot-yourself trick. We even got one of us kissing. . . . And he picked which ones he wanted me to send him. That was so cool—my whole tummy squiggled then. And felt a bit sick at the same time, because soon it would come to an end.

The whole day had been so perfect that I even forgot

that I was in the outback and that there were still nasty beasties who had a hit contract out on me. Even when I slipped off to find a tree.

All day there'd only been one thing that'd worried me. One time after Mitch and I kissed, I'd looked up to see Callie watching us, and I caught her expression just before she dived under the water. She looked hurt, and I could see why. It isn't fun when someone comes in and takes your best friend away—and I figured that living so far away from everyone, that was how they'd feel about each other.

I'd talk to her about it. I'd tell her it was okay—that I understood, that she'd still be his best friend. Unless . . .

Oh, no.

Of course . . .

The thought hit like a landslide and was why I'd totally zoned out to everything around me.

Mitch's voice finally reached me. It seemed to come from a long way away. I started to smile. . . . His tone was soft and low, but as the words became clearer, I also heard the worry. "Maddie. Don't turn around. I want you to get down low. Lie flat. Do it now."

"What?" Well, like, hello! What's the first thing you do if someone says, 'Don't turn around'? I mean, it's second nature! Everybody does it—I would not believe I was the only one!

So I did. And my heart stopped for probably the absolute final time.

There it was.

This time I wasn't being a drama queen—this time

167

everything I felt was totally real, and I knew all the times I'd been scared through my life had just been a practice for the real thing. This was the real thing. I truly felt the blood drain from my face.

It was big and gray and snarky. And it was coming at me pretty fast. Who said they were slow on land? My vision was blurred. Tears? Sweat? My scream didn't help—I swear, its eyes got beadier. Meaner. Sweat ran down my back and even over my shoulders; I tried to run but it felt like I was hopping up and down on the spot like some brainless cartoon character. Oh, God! I tried! I could hear my own breathing, my own heartbeat thundering. . . .

Someone yelled for Mitch. It was a horrible, bloodcurdling cry that I barely recognized as my own. My sobs were gasps, and I was forgetting how to breathe. Over and over and over in my head all I could see was the death roll.

Voices yelled back at me. Words. I couldn't make them out. I just kept backing up to the tree, hoping this monster would slow up. . . . But the tree seemed so far away . . . and the big, horrible, ugly thing kept coming at me.

At the last moment I turned and sprinted, but I was too late. I felt my foot snagged—then it had me. I fought and screamed—it held so tight! It was wrapped around me. I couldn't get free! "Please! Please . . ." It was smothering me, pressing me down. . . . I waited for the teeth—and tensed myself against it. The first would be the worst—after that maybe I'd pass out. . . . "Oh please let me pass out. . . ."

"Madeline! Stop! It's me!"

The voice kind of penetrated and I slowed. Maybe I was hallucinating. . . . It came again. "It's me, honey. It's me. . . ."

I opened my eyes and looked into Mitch's brilliant blue eyes. He was lying fully on top of me, his legs wrapped around me. My whole body was shuddering—I couldn't stop. . . . Everything hurt so much. "Oh, Mitch . . . !"

And I stopped fighting—and just sobbed.

It was like floodwaters had opened up, and nothing could stop them. My breaths were noisy gasps that jerked in and out. Pain came in waves and seemed to roll like the ground we were lying on.

I couldn't speak; couldn't tell him. Through it all he just held me and kissed my forehead, over and over whispering that everything was okay.

When I'd stopped shaking so much, he slowly moved off me. "Are you okay, Maddie? Does it hurt anywhere?"

"E-everywhere. Something hurts bad. . . ."

He looked up at the others, who'd moved closer. I heard Callie's sobs and felt her hands stroking mine. Jace looked stunned, all pale and frightened. "Cal, get the blanket out of the saddlebag; Jace, get the first-aid kit."

He ran his hands down my body. At any other time it might have felt great—today it just hurt. My left arm was beneath me and I saw him look really worried. "I'm going to have to move you, mate. Okay?"

I know he meant to be gentle, and I know he was—but as soon as he started to lift me I screamed all over again. "Oh, God—I think I'm going to puke. . . ." He held me till it was over and then he kissed me so gently. And I tasted his tears. . . .

I was flat on my back now and still the pain hadn't stopped. The others had run back—I felt their footsteps rumble through the ground. The rug went around me and was tucked in tight. Mitch stared at my arm; then his eyes were darting around the area, searching.

"Is it bad?"

His eyes held mine. "Yep, mate—it's bad."

I didn't need proof. I'd just seen the faces of the other two. I think Jace barfed.

Callie gave me water. Mitch really worried over the splint. He'd sent her for some sturdy bark pieces that he curved in tight around my arm from the elbow down and then he bound it over and over with bandages from the first-aid kit. He said the bone wasn't through, but it had completely moved. It hurt like crazy, but in a weird, removed way, I knew he was helping me.

Saying anything else took a while, and even then I could barely make myself say the word I knew had to come out. "The crocodile?"

He shook his head and stroked some hair out of my eyes. "Croc? Ohhh, jeez, Maddie. It wasn't a crocodile—it was a goanna. A lizard. Like an iguana . . . Remember

we talked about them before? It was a big fella. Huge—
but it wasn't going to eat you; it was afraid."

"But you sounded—"

His voice rumbled over me, soothing me. "Yeah, I
know. And I'm so sorry." He sighed. "It just happened so
fast. You must have startled it, and it was trying to get to
the tree. When they're scared they have to get high. If you
were the highest thing between it and the tree it'd climb
up you! And, mate, those claws would rip you to pieces.
Especially a big bloke like that; they'd be like carving
knives. I turned around just in time to see it taking off after you. I just wanted you to get down. Actually, it's pretty
rare for them to go after anyone like that. I only saw it
once before, when someone got between a mum and her
kids. I'd say there are babies around here somewhere."

"If I'd listened . . ." I licked my dry lips. "Did it get me?"

"Caught your ankle. By then I'd thrown myself over
you in case it ran over you."

"Did it get you?"

"Nah. Just a bit of a scratch on my back." My eyelids
were fluttering back down when I saw Callie flick him a
look. He sort of ignored it, and then they made plans to
get me back.

Mitch carried me to the bike and propped me up on
the front and tucked in real close behind me. My arm
was in a sling but I was too out-of-it to know much else.
I remembered his arms coming around me and the bike
starting up; I remembered leaning back into his chest,
and then it was a blur.

Next I remembered being carried to Mitch's room. Other people were there. At one stage I opened my eyes and looked up at a kind face; she was bathing my forehead. She smiled at me and I tried to smile back. She was stunning. And so much like Callie I didn't have to guess who she was. Callie was going to be just like that . . . beautiful . . .

I don't know how many hours I drifted in and out, but next there were nurses there. A doctor too. They moved my arm and I puked again. They gave me an injection and the pain started to go away.

I heard them say, "Darwin Hospital," and then I was being wheeled on a trolley outside.

Callie ran over and hugged me; she was still crying. "Oh, Maddie . . ."

I tried to smile. "Don't cry. I'm going to miss you. . . . Will you come to New York one day?" She nodded, and then I remembered. "Oh, Cal . . . I'm so sorry. I worked it out. Mitch's the one, isn't he? The one you like? I'm such an idiot."

She leaned down and hugged me. "It's Mitch's choice, Maddie. And if it's not me, then I'm glad it's you."

Yeah, right. I watched her walk away and I wasn't so tranquilized that I didn't know how much that had hurt. That was one gutsy girl.

More wooziness kicked in, and when Mitch came up next it was like he was swaying. His shirt was off and he was walking kinda stiff. Geez! I hoped he hadn't put his back out lifting me. Had I said that out loud? My head was really starting to spin.

He had shadows under his eyes, but there was that same lazy smile. "Not exactly the farewell I had planned for us. . . ."

Even in my woozy-headed state my heart still leaped up and tried to get out. "You planned something?"

He nodded—and winked. This time my heart cha-chaed to the other side of my body!

"You saved my life today, Mitch." My mouth felt like it was filled with cotton wool. "T-Thank you."

He closed his eyes, suddenly looking like he was the one who should be going to the hospital. "No, don't thank me." He squeezed my good hand tighter and looked at me again. "Jeez, Maddie. I don't think any of us realized how tough this week has been on you, mate. And you've been such a flamin' good sport about the whole thing. . . . You're pretty amazing, you know that? It was only when I saw you fall apart that I realized that you've really been through hell."

"It wasn't all bad." I tried to grin.

He didn't smile. "I broke your arm, Maddie. It was my fault."

"What? So now you think I'm gonna break every time you jump on me?" The woozy stuff was making me brave.

"Maddie . . . !" The word came out on a gurgle; I'd seen that breath he almost choked on. I heard the warning too.

"I know. I know . . . I'm only fifteen."

He bent down now, stiffly and slowly, and I wanted to ask about his back. But then he kissed me—and I forgot. . . .

"You won't always be fifteen. . . ."

Okay—now I needed oxygen. A whole tank!

The doctor turned back to me again then. "Sorry, kids. It's time to go." He patted Mitch on the shoulder. "Take care of that, Mitch. Maddie? We're going to have to wheel you on this trolley for a little while. It'll be a bit rough, but we'll try to pick the flattest path. With Stan away with the ute, we got the bird in as close as we could."

Bird? Nothing made sense. "Jace?" Where was Jace?

As the trolley moved forward, I watched the people who walked behind. Two nurses walked beside me. Everyone was looking like they do in crazy mirrors. Mitch was at the end, helping push. I think someone told him not to, but he shrugged them off. I couldn't see where I was going, but that didn't matter. It was who and what I was leaving behind that mattered. They were the memories I wanted printed on my brain. And I needed to see Jace. . . .

But I was fading fast.

Suddenly we all stopped and I understood. A plane? Across the side I saw words. They were blurry, but I finally made them out: *Royal Flying Doctor Service.* How totally cool was that! What a great thing to do—fly out to help people who were miles from anywhere.

They loaded me in, and probably just in time, because my eyelids were too heavy, and I couldn't fight it any longer. Still, I stretched for one last look at Mitch. I needed to see Mitch. And Callie. And . . .

"No, wait!" The words were slurred but I had to make them understand. His face swam back into my mind. So pale. So scared. I couldn't leave him here! He was my responsibility, and he'd be so scared. His mom was taken away in an ambulance. . . . I had to make sure he was okay. *Wanted* to make sure he was okay. "I can't go. I can't go without my brother. . . . Jace?"

The crowd cleared and his face was there in front of me. "Jace? I need you to come with me, bro. I can't do this alone."

His eyes were red and he looked like crap. Actually, he looked like a lost kid.

"Will you come with me, mate?"

He nodded and I saw Callie and Mitch grin at each other as they pushed him on board. He came straight up and sat beside my head. I looked over and grinned. I think it was lopsided.

His hand landed on my shoulder. "Are you gonna be all right, Mad?"

"I'll be back giving you hell before you know it, Brat. Enjoy the vacation while you can."

This time he smiled. Really smiled. And he relaxed. That was great, 'cause I could not hold these peepers open one more second. *Hasta la vista.*

The next few hours were a bit of a blur, which was

probably a good thing. In my hospital room I'd been dozing on and off. I only had to stay overnight, and I'd lost track, but I figured it was probably somewhere in the early hours of the next day already.

The thought of it made me feel empty—which was totally weird. I'd be going to some hotel to wait for Mom and Barry—and, hey, this could only be a good thing, right? Air-con, waitstaff, plumbing . . .

But there would be no Mitch . . . or Callie. . . .

A wave of pain hit and I tried to get more comfortable. Even though they'd reset the bone and put a cast on my arm, it still hurt a lot. They'd promised I'd feel a bit better by tomorrow.

But right now it wasn't. It was aching. And I had ugly fingers. Five fat sausages that looked like they'd been filled with blue-veined cheese. Eeeeooww. Scratch blue-veined cheese off my list of preferred foods. At this rate I'd be on bread and water. Well, at least I could make the bread!

More pain. I didn't remember groaning, but I must have, because suddenly someone beside me was offering help.

Chapter Eleven

"Barry? What are you doing here? Where's Mom?"

He smiled and reached out to touch my cheek. It was a kind thing to do. The sort of thing a dad would do. Probably. How would I know?

"Your mum got some phone calls from the office just as we were leaving to come here. You know they'd only call if it was an emergency. . . . Apparently people will lose their jobs unless she can fix this. She's checked into the hotel—I told her to take care of it and I'd shoot on over here and check on you. She'll come as soon as she's through."

"Oh." My head was buzzing in circles; I felt like a plane that couldn't find a place to land. My mom didn't come? "Sure. Okay. Um . . . how d-did you get here? What about the car?"

He was watching me closely. "She loves you, Madeline. She was so distraught that she couldn't get here—I had to force her to stay and take care of her work staff. I told her I was here and she didn't have to do it all alone. . . . Believe me, she fell apart when she heard the news. I didn't ever expect to see that—and I have to say, it was kind of nice." He reached down to a bag. "Oh, by the way, I grabbed some magazines at the newsstand out front. I hope they're okay. I had a devil of a time choosing the right ones. . . ."

Barbie magazine? The Ashley and Mary-Kate magazine? Ooohh, boy . . . There were so many things I could have said at that moment. So many opportunities—but I said none of them. Instead I smiled. And thanked him. He didn't have to buy me anything. In fact, the way I'd treated him, it was a wonder he was even here at all. And even then I'd probably have a weak courtroom defense if he'd just barged in and held a pillow over my head!

He'd probably get an award!

He was right about Mom too. This was the mom I knew and loved. Even though she didn't come right over, she did love me. I've never doubted that—well, maybe just for that one second—and I knew she worked hard for us to give me the life she wanted to give me. And sure, I loved it. I was the Park Avenue princess, wasn't I?

But even though I'd never admitted it, just sometimes I wished she wanted to give me less—that way I'd get to see her more often. But I guess the bottom line was, I was proud of her. No one had handed my mom anything. She'd worked for it all.

That meant she was important. Okay—so I couldn't have it all. But at least I had a mom who really loved me. Some people weren't that lucky.

"So how did you get here?"

Barry smiled. "That bush radio of theirs. It's amazing. As soon as news came through to us we had people calling from everywhere offering help. One family was on their way back up here to Darwin, and they picked us up and brought us with them. Stan's taken the part back, and he and his partner have offered to fix it. That's the sort of people they are. . . ."

"I know."

He looked across at Jace sleeping on the bed next to mine in my semiprivate suite. "I heard you did a bit of fixing yourself. The hospital said they've never seen anything like it. You in here demanding a room with two beds—so there'd be one for your 'brother.' "

"It was more smoke than fire." I shrugged. "I just wanted to make sure he was okay, and to do that I had to have him with me. He's had a hard day. He was pretty scared. . . . I think it brought back some memories he probably didn't need dug up."

Barry stood and leaned over me then. "That was very intuitive, Madeline." For the first time I noticed a few tears pooling in his eyes. "Thank you." And then he kissed me. Just a peck. Another dad thing. . . .

While he was up he checked on Jace, who was sleeping like a baby. He was probably loving this air-con! "Don't let me keep you awake, will you? I'll just stretch out in this armchair till your mum arrives. I'd like to be here for Jason as well—although I certainly can't complain about his care so far."

I grinned a sleepy grin. "Hey? Wanna bed? I bet I can get you one."

He laughed softly. "I have no doubt you could. . . . No doubt at all."

As I drifted off again, I knew that somewhere Barry and I had arrived at a truce. He was an okay guy. . . .

Just . . . why did he have to live in Australia?

It was so good to wake up and find Mom asleep in a chair beside my bed. She looked up and smiled. She looked like crap—my designer mum all crumpled and disheveled. But, hey, it was just so good to see her. She must have been thinking the same thing.

"How did you get stripy orange hair?"

"Long story. It's getting better. You look great, Mom."

She got up and hugged me. "So do you, punkin."

Now there was a memory. . . . "'Punkin'? Gee, Mom—that's a blast from the past." For someone who hadn't cried in forever, I was finding it mighty easy all of a sudden. That darned lump raced back into position, and I was doing my usual tricks to melt it away.

And then I stopped trying, because Mom was standing there in front me doing exactly what I was trying not to do. She was crying. I'd never seen her cry—and when

I was a little kid I decided that if she didn't cry, then I wouldn't.

Now we both were, and it felt great.

I wiped her face with a tissue in my good hand. "Did you make any decisions? Like with you and Barry? It's just that . . . well . . . everything you've done in your life . . . I think you've done for me." I shrugged. "Maybe you should do something for you. You're not getting any younger, Mom."

She took a pretend swipe at me, but she was laughing. "Thank you. That means a lot." Then she paused. "Barry and I . . . well we've decided we're still getting married, but there's no rush. Neither of us is quite prepared to uproot and move just at this moment. But we're going to spend as much time as we can together. I think we can afford a few more vacations down under— what do you think?"

"I get to see more of Jace? Great! Oh, Mom—we're going to have our hands so full! That kid is going to be Lady-Killer Central. And if Dee is his twin, it's going to take all of us to keep them in line!"

"So," she said, smiling, "you're not completely against having younger siblings?"

"Specific ones are okay." I smiled but as I watched her it faded. This was about more than just siblings. "Mom? Like, is this wait thing what you *really* want to do? Because, like, I'm totally cool. . . ."

"It is, Madeline. It's what Barry and I both want, and it's for a lot of reasons—careers, families. . . . And it's not forever. We've given ourselves four years, maybe less if we can work things out before then. Besides, in two years you'll be off to college anyway, and who knows where you'll end up?"

"Speaking of that, I was wondering about the U of WA?"

Mom's eyebrows nearly went AWOL. She'd been trying to get me to talk about colleges for two years. "U of WA?"

"University of Western Australia."

"I see. Do they offer a good program?"

"Dunno. But they attract great students."

"Ahhh. The slow parent suddenly comprehends. How did that go, anyway?"

I felt the color rush to my cheeks. "It was amazing. . . ."

She groaned out loud, and the Brat stirred. "And here you are telling me we're going to have our hands full with Jason and Dee! All I can say is that at least I'll have had plenty of practice!"

"Oh, bite me, Mom!" I grinned. It felt good to be back with her.

Barry and Jace left the hospital as soon as he woke up (the hospital demanded their bed back! How rude!), but I had to wait to be discharged. I'd have been just glad to get out of the place, but when the cab pulled up in front of a five-star hotel, it did feel good.

"I was so totally born for this."

"Unfortunately, Madeline, so was I. . . . Let's go have

a spa! Oh, wait—maybe you can't do that with your arm in that cast. . . ."

"Don't torture me, Mom."

Mom and Barry had a three-bedroom suite up near the top floor, but I didn't look at anything but my bathroom. Yes, it had plumbing. I could relax.

We had shopping to do, and it was totally legitimate—most of our clothes were back down at Mitch's property. But after that . . . well, it got a bit boring.

It was worse for me because I couldn't swim. I did get a new bikini—a hot-pink-and-orange swirl. Very cool. Very Australian chic. I even found one with a bit of padding. . . . I brought Pattie and Reesa up-to-date and found out the latest gossip—like that Shelley and Josh were now a couple. (Aha! Now the lingerie gift made sense. It was a guilt gift! Oh, who cared! Shelley was beating herself up for no reason—I figured they deserved each other! Besides, with the friends I'd made down here, she'd just dropped to at least tenth on my friend list. Maybe lower . . .)

And I got my journal up to date. Wow—there was a fair bit to report. Writing it *did* cause me a few blushable moments. Like—how far did you actually go in a journal that you wanted your dad to read? Would he be cool about it—like happy that I was normal? Or would he freak and want to slap me in chains till I was forty? I guess it depended on if I actually met the guy before I was forty. . . .

And if he cared.

Maybe there'd be some things I'd leave out. . . .

But after that we just sat around the pool for a few days; in truth both Jace and I were a bit lost.

All day long we'd say stuff like, "Back at Mitch's we'd be doing this now." Or, "Wonder what Mitch and Callie are doing?"

Actually, that thought kept me busier than anything else. I'd made a decision. Okay, this was the new Madeline. I had decided that Mitch and Callie were perfect for each other. Yes, I know. That meant I was going to have to give him up. Walk away. But it was for the best. He wanted a wife who loved the outback, and she did. And she was nice.

Of course, I cried buckets. I mean, this could have been the only one true love of my life—and there was no mistake, I was in love! I only had to think of him and every part of me went to Jell-O. The guy was everything I'd ever wanted—except that he lived in the wrong place and didn't want to leave!

I stayed awake at night reliving those kisses. I looked for his smile in every guy in the hotel. And sometimes it just hurt so much and I would give anything to hear his voice or have him send one of those winks. . . .

But it was never going to work. Pattie had a needle-point that said, *If you love something set it free.*

That's what I had to do.

I could see it all.

It would go like this: Mitch and I would have to meet up sometime in our near future. I would hold his hands and look deeply into his eyes. My tears would fall in fat drops, leaving big watery marks on my cool new Dolce & Gabbana shirt-and-skirt ensemble.

I would tell him to go to Callie. That she was the one for him. And he'd beg and wail and plead with me to reconsider. But I'd stand firm. Callie was for him. . . . He had to see it. And so, with a totally broken heart, he would go to Callie, who would eventually (but not too fast) heal it.

Me? I would die a childless old maid—lonely (except for my seventeen cats) but not bitter. I would know in my heart I had done one great service to the man I love.

It would be my one big selfless act: I'd give him away. . . . I'd write a book about it. They'd make a movie. Britney Spears would play me.

I blew my nose hard. It would be the toughest thing I would ever do. I had to be strong. Firm. The only good thing was that I would refuse to do this over the telephone or e-mail and *never* over that blasted radio—and that meant I had oh, at least two years to sweat it. Until then I'd just miss him like crazy. . . .

"Nice tan."

"Whaaa?" I swear, only the anchor tied to my left arm kept me from falling off my lounge chair. "Mitch!" Was it a mirage? Oh, man! He was gorgeous. Was it possible for someone to grow more gorgeous in three days? I couldn't stop staring at him. . . . "Are you real?"

He laughed and squatted down so he was at my level. "Yeah, I'm real. How's the arm?"

That voice. That lazy smile . . . "Arm? What arm? Oh! You mean my broken arm! Depression fracture. That's why it looked so bad. They've reset it. Got to wear this baby for about eight weeks."

All the while I was speaking, he was staring at me really hard. Like he hadn't heard anything I'd said. "I've missed you like hell, Maddie."

Oxygen jammed somewhere halfway to my lungs. "Me too . . ."

"Can I kiss you? Is it okay?"

I nodded. Oh, baby—just try not doing it!

And he did.

And someone turned the world off.

"Ahem . . . yoo-hoo!"

Slowly we drifted apart, and I blinked as I looked up into my mother's eyes. Those eyebrows were missing in action again. Well, hey, it's not like she thinks I haven't been kissed—she just hadn't actually seen me *at it* before. Barry was behind her, and he was grinning like a chimpanzee. But at least I didn't pick up any bad vibes. . . .

Mitch rose slowly and shook hands with Mom and Barry. They were really pleased to see him and couldn't stop thanking him and his dad for all their help. Apparently Mitch had brought the car back.

Jace came rushing out of the pool. His face was brighter than any Christmas tree I'd seen all season. "Mitch!" He hurled himself, and Mitch caught him and pretended to throw a few punches. Guy stuff.

"How's your back?" That was my mom.

"Your back?" I saw Mitch and Jace dart a look at each other. My heart started another one of those deep thumping campaigns. "What's with your back?"

He shrugged. "Great." To me he said, "It was nothing. . . ."

Like I believed that!

"Nonsense," said Mom, who isn't known for her tact. "You got sutures, didn't you? Something about wrestling a giant lizard?"

"Mitch?" Tears had come from nowhere and were flying everywhere! I couldn't stop them.

He squatted back to me. "I promise it wasn't that bad, Mad. . . ."

"Am I missing something here?" Mom asked.

Jace sighed. "Mitch probably saved Maddie's life." He told us the entire story—this time not missing the parts that had been left out before. "When Mitch threw himself over Maddie, the goanna was in full flight and just kept on and went straight over Mitch. He got twenty sutures. Maddie, when he was trying to brace your arm, he had all this blood pouring out of his back. And he wouldn't let me or Callie help bring you home. He had to do it all. He wouldn't let anyone look at him till you'd been fixed up. He swore us to secrecy, too."

"Mitch? No!"

"It's okay, mate." And then he was holding me again. Man, I had so much to get my head around. . . .

Mom just stood there staring at us. She looked gray.

Finally she blinked and pulled herself together. "Well, it seems you two got past forgetting each other's names. . . ."

I actually giggled then. Poor Mom. She had a lot to think about. And almost losing me was just one of them. And I think it was the other one that sent her into the biggest spin. I'd explain it all to her later—and tell her she didn't have anything to worry about. Yet . . .

Mom and Barry treated Mitch to a few days in Darwin till it was time for our flight back; he shared a room with Jace, who was stoked to have his roommate back. For Mitch and me . . . well, it was great to be together, but Mom made sure we didn't get much time alone. Which, if it hadn't been so infuriating, was almost hilarious. Poor Barry—he should never think about a career on the stage. Mom had him on the case, and everywhere we were, so was he. He tried so hard to be cool, but he was so obvious. . . .

On the last morning we sneaked off for a walk. All night I'd eaten myself up over Callie and what to do. And as much as I loved Mitch, I figured it was time. . . .

"You okay? This is our last time together for who knows how long, you know."

I sighed. *Here goes.* "Maybe longer than you think . . . Mitch, I have to say something. It's killing me, but I want you to see it as the gift it is. . . ."

"What?"

"Don't be like that! This is really hard for me! Do you

think it's easy to tell the guy you love that you think he should be with someone else?"

"*What!*"

"Oh—hang on—I didn't mean to blurt it all out like that. I had this whole scene in my head where you beg and plead and I am noble and strong and you beg more and I won't budge and then you walk off into the sunset. . . ."

"Are you drinking enough water?"

"Oh, stop with the water! You want it in English?"

"Please."

This was it. "Mitch, I think you should marry Callie." There, it was done. I braced myself and waited for him to beg and plead. Then I would move into phase two.

"*I don't.*"

I held up my good hand. "What? No, hang on. . . . That's not how it goes. . . . You see, I think Callie is perfect for you. Much more perfect than me, and I think—"

He grabbed my good hand and pulled me to him. That was a low blow—how was I supposed to think now?! "Madeline Frances Flannagan, I take you to be my . . ."

My heart stopped!

". . . girlfriend, forsaking all others."

Girlfriend? Oh, that's right. There were just one or two steps to consider before marriage. But *girlfriend*, huh? Hey, that was cool. Yes, that was very cool. And *pfft!* All this selflessness wasn't what it was cracked up to be anyway. I didn't even like cats!

"I do! And Mitchell Stanley (yerk) Maloney, I take you to be my forever man. My totally cool knight in shining armor, my savior, forsaking all others."

"I do. . . . Can we seal it with a kiss?"

"Better make it one to last a long time. . . ."

And I think he did. I knew I wouldn't be forgetting it in a hurry.

When we walked back to the hotel he got this really cheeky look on his face. "I gotta ask you—did you really think I proposed to you on that first night?"

"Oh, duh! Of course not! As if!"

He burst out laughing. "You did!"

"Did not. When did you first know you loved me and couldn't live without me?"

"First time? First shower. I realized then that I hadn't laughed so hard in a long time. Big-time? Dancing in the rain . . . when you laughed. What about you?"

"When you pulled up in the pickup . . . Did you really forget my name? Answer carefully."

We'd reached the hotel where Mom and Barry were waiting with all our bags. Mitch looked across at them, and the mood changed. "No, I didn't. Last question. When will I see you again?"

That one stopped me. "I don't know. . . . It could be a long time, Mitch. Couple of years even . . ."

He nodded. "What happens if—"

"We find someone else? Then I think we just have to be honest. Oh! I just remembered that last part of that

190

sampler! 'If you love something, set it free. If it comes back to you, it's yours.' "

His smile was sad as he pulled me into a big hug. "In that case," he whispered, "go free, beautiful Madeline, so you can come back to me."

And then he was gone.

And I knew I hadn't left a teeny part of my heart in the outback—I'd left it all. . . .

Come to the Never Never and you'll never never want to leave. . . .

Back in Sydney we saw all the sights, and I should have been totally jazzed because it's an über groovy city. Kind of like a mini New York, actually. But I just couldn't get into it.

At the airport Mom's farewell to Barry was almost as soppy as mine to Mitch. Then it hit me. . . . Omigod, my mother and I were both in long distance relationships. We'd be able to swap boyfriend stories, teach each other Australian, and spend our Saturday nights making fudge (or maybe damper bush bread?) and remembering the good old days.

Waaahhhh! Someone save me from sappy plots and bad style. . . .

We'd become the Gilmore Girls!

That slightly depressing thought weighing me down, I snuggled into my seat as best I could with this dumb cast on. It was going to be a long flight, but I had a lot of memories to keep me occupied. . . .

Kaz Delaney

And a lot of plans to make. For starters, trying to find the perfect bridesmaid color to suit both Callie and Reesa was probably going to take me years!

After that I'd start on the guest list. . . .

Then work out the names of our children.

I wonder how Mitch would feel about "Bruce"?

Of course, I still had to add the last few days to my journal. There was a thought! Maybe I'd name my first son after him? After my dad? Oops. Freeze that thought. . . . That'd mean I'd also have to call him Stanley after Mitch's dad—yerk. On second thought, maybe I'd just stick with Bruce. . . .

❄ Kaz Delaney ❄
My Life as a Snow Bunny

LERVE: LOVE WITH A SWISS ACCENT

It can: ❄

✔ Warm up the chilly ski slopes.
Who knew Colorado was Hunk Heaven? Not Jo Vincent.

✔ Provide a fun distraction.
It's not like Jo's going to get any attention from her dad. He brought his own après-ski entertainment—her name is Kate.

✔ Happen with Hans.
Every girl should experience one in her life: a Swiss guy as smooth as chocolate and just as sweet . . .
So European! So regal! So mysterious! Like . . .
❄   what's all this stuff about kangaroos?

The Year My Life Went Down the Loo
by Katie Maxwell

Subject: The Grotty and the Fabu (No, it's not a song.)
From: Mrs.Oded@btelecom.co.uk
To: Dru@seattlegrrl.com

Things That Really Irk My Pickle About Living in England

• The school uniform

• Piddlington-on-the-weld (I will forever be known as Emily from *Piddlesville*)

• Marmite (It's yeast sludge! GACK!)

• The ghost in my underwear drawer (Spectral hands fondling my bras—enough said!)

• No malls! What are these people *thinking???*

Things That Keep Me From Flying Home to Seattle for Good Coffee

• Aidan (*Hunkalicious!*)

• Devon (*Droolworthy?* Understatement of the year!*)

• Fang (He puts the *num* in *nummy!*)

• Holly (Any girl who hunts movie stars with me—and Oded Fehr *will be mine*—is a friend for life.)

• Über-coolio Polo Club (Where the snogging is FINE!)

They Wear WHAT Under Their Kilts?

by Katie Maxwell

Subject: Emily's Glossary for People Who Haven't Been to Scotland
From: Mrs.Legolas@kiltnet.com
To: Dru@seattlegrrl.com

Faffing about: running around doing nothing. In other words, spending a month supposedly doing work experience on a Scottish sheep farm, but really spending days on Kilt Watch at the nearest castle.

Schottie: Scottish Hottie, also known as Ruaraidh.

Mad schnoogles: the British way of saying big smoochy kisses. Will admit it sounds v. smart to say it that way.

Bunch of yobbos: a group of mindless idiots. In Scotland, can also mean sheep.

Stooshie: uproar, as in, "If Holly thinks she can take Ruaraidh from me without causing a stooshie, she's out of her mind!"

Sheep dip: not an appetizer.

YOU ARE *SO* CURSED!

NAOMI NASH

High school's a dog eat dog world, but Vickie Marotti has an edge. Scorned by the jocks and cheerleaders? Misunderstood by the uptight vice principal? No problem. Not when you're an adept street magician, hexing bullies who dare harass you or your outcast friends!

But then cute and popular upperclassman Gio Carson recognizes the truth: Vick's no more a witch than she is class president. Her dark curses are nothing more than smoke and mirrors. Will he tell the world, or will it be their little secret? Vick's about to learn a valuable lesson: that real magic lies in knowing your true friends.

Didn't want this book to end?

There's more waiting at **www.smoochya.com**:

Win FREE books and makeup!
Read excerpts from other books!
Chat with the authors!
Horoscopes!
Quizzes!

 Bringing you the books on everyone's lips!